The evening was turning to night when he arrived at the factory, and cars were turning on their headlights, but the air was still warm, and groups of drinkers were taking their leisure outside the pubs in the Old Kent Road.

Trace undid the padlock on the tall factory gates, pulled them open and drove the car into the courtyard. Only after he had closed the gates behind him could he relax and light one of the rare Marlboros he allowed himself.

The woman was still asleep in the back of the Ford, snoring gently, her head on one shoulder. A thin line of silver drool ran from the corner of her mouth to the lapel of her jacket.

Trace grimaced in disgust as he undid the seat belt and carried her into the building. People. He hated them.

JIM BALLANTYNE

THE TORTURER

GOLLANCZ HORROR

GOLLANCZ HORROR
First published in Great Britain 1995
as a paperback original
by Victor Gollancz
An imprint of the Cassell Group
Wellington House, 125 Strand, London WC2R 0BB

A catalogue record for this book is
available from the British Library.

ISBN 0 575 05228 7

Typeset by CentraCet Ltd, Cambridge
Printed and bound in Great Britain
by Cox & Wyman Ltd, Reading, Berks

For Robyn

1947–1995

It's all like a dream to me now.

1

A few years earlier it would have been described as a yuppie bar. Now, God knows how you'd describe it. It was on the edge of the City of London, close to Tower Bridge, and a faint odour of the river crept through the windows that were open to dispel the body heat of the people gathered there on the evening of a late June dealing day.

It was noisy inside. The chatter from the hundred or so customers grew louder as the hour got later and the alcohol intake increased, and rose above the clink of glass on glass, and the clatter of feet on the parquet floor, all overlaid by the bass boom from the Phil Collins album on the CD jukebox amplified through half a dozen huge wall-mounted speakers.

But the corner table that Matt Trace had taken for himself seemed locked in a cone of silence. No one disturbed his solitude by taking either of the vacant seats beside him, and if their eyes skidded across him, they soon moved away to some other object of interest.

Not that Matt wasn't attractive. He was. When he wanted to be, he could be the most attractive and charming man on earth. But when he didn't, as he didn't at that moment, there was something about him that made other people keep their distance.

He was aged somewhere between thirty and thirty-five, and tall. More than six feet. With a muscular and athletic body that he kept at peak fitness. He was handsome, too. With long, black hair, and a face that often reminded people of a young Burt Lancaster. But his eyes could be cold, and he rarely smiled. That day he was dressed in a faded blue denim shirt and tight black jeans. On the back of his chair hung an expensive Schott leather jacket that gleamed in the late evening sunset.

He was very still sitting there, and he fancied he could almost hear the hiss of the bubbles from the Kirin beer that sat untouched in the glass in front of him. He eased his feet in their Timberland loafers, and from behind the slightly mirrored frames of his Porsche sunglasses he eyed his target.

She was sitting with a group of work colleagues at a table overlooking the flat expanse of the Thames. They were talking animatedly, and drinking champagne as fast as the bottles could be brought to the table. As he looked at them, so confident in their youth and vitality, he thought of the old rhyme: All golden lads and lassies must, like chimney sweepers, come to dust.

To all intents and purposes Matt could have been a love-sick suitor gazing at the object of his desire. But there was no tenderness in his gaze. Just the sort of interest a scientist might have for a specimen he was studying under a microscope.

And although they had never met, he knew more about her than any of the men she occasionally took home for the night to her flat.

She was twenty-six years old. Twenty-seven in exactly eighty-three days' time. She was five foot seven inches tall, and weighed a few ounces short of nine stone. Her hair was blonde. Natural. Her vital statistics were thirty-six, twenty-seven, thirty-six. She was allergic to certain kinds of seafood, and had a birthmark on her right hip. He knew a lot more about her, and he ran the stats through his mind as he watched her. Briefly he wondered just what she did or had done that had brought them both to this exact spot, but then dismissed the thought as irrelevant. He had received his instructions in one of the many and varied ways that they arrived, and the transfer of his fee had been paid into the overseas bank of his choice some weeks previously.

It was always thus. Trace had his network of contacts, diligently built up over the years. Contacts who owed him, or who had skeletons rattling in cupboards to which Trace had the keys.

And now he was ready for his latest job. He knew exactly what would happen next. Within the next couple of hours she would leave. The transmitter he had placed on her Golf GTi Cabriolet still nestled snugly against the metal under the back bumper, and the receiver mounted on the dash of his Sierra Cosworth was working perfectly. He wondered if she'd leave alone, or if she was feeling randy and would take someone along. If she did, he'd follow her to see if she took him back to her home, or just went for a meal and then dropped him off. Not that that was likely. When she was hot, she was hot; as the tapes he had of her telephone calls, and the audio and video evidence from the tiny camera he'd hidden in her apartment in the high security block in Battersea showed.

High security. That was a laugh, he thought. A few

incompetent or past-it blokes in tea-stained paramilitary uniforms with some ridiculous corporate logo on the shoulder, and a two-way radio for company, imagining they were keeping the criminal hordes at bay outside.

Matt had solutions for all that. In the old smelting factory he rented in Peckham, and occasionally lived in, he had three Transit vans. They were painted in the livery of Telecom, British Gas, and London Electricity. Plus a Volvo ambulance and a Ford Mondeo police ARV. He had uniforms to conform with each vehicle. Plus a filing cabinet that was full of security passes in various names for almost any corporation in the country, and every known government institution. There was hardly a building in Britain that he could not infiltrate. The block in Battersea had been a piece of cake.

He had managed to repair one of the giant burners at the factory, so that any incriminating evidence could be swiftly destroyed. And there had been a lot of that lately. His mouth twisted at the thought. But not the bodies. The bodies he left for others to find. That way his status inside the underworld grew, and his commissions multiplied. His reputation was first class, and he was proud of it and the fear it engendered in others. Only once had he made a mistake. The thought displeased him, so he put it to the back of his mind. He continued to watch the young woman, whom he would soon know more intimately still.

He looked at her and her friends talking to each other, mouthing words he couldn't hear. He could easily have bugged the table too, for it was one they regularly used. But what would have been the point? He was hardly interested in their mundane conversation about shares and money prices. No. He could wait a few more hours or even days, when he could have her for his own and begin to practise his unique profession on her.

2

After two more bottles of Moët had been delivered to the table and consumed, the girl made her tipsy farewells and left. Alone.

Fine, thought Trace, and after a minute or so he followed, snaking through the crowd as if it didn't exist.

Outside it was still hot, and the setting sun sat on the edges of the buildings on the other side of the river like a giant blood orange.

Trace went to the Cosworth and activated the receiver mounted beneath the dashboard. The speaker bleeped softly. A red light on the map of central London that appeared on the screen began to move in a westerly direction.

Home, he thought. Perfect. But not tonight, my sweet. He switched on the ignition. The exhaust rumbled menacingly as he blipped the accelerator, put the car into gear and, reversing neatly out of his parking space, followed.

A giant crow sat on the edge of the roof of the bar building, pecking at the hind leg of a dead rat. When the crow saw the black Ford pull out of the parking lot, it dropped its snack and, with a clatter of wings, flew off in the direction of the setting sun.

Trace drove slowly along the embankment, one eye on the road, the other on the red dot that moved across the digital map. Yes. Home, he thought, and driving within the speed limit because you're a bit pissed. So predictable. He put his foot down, and the Sierra's powerful turbo-charged engine responded sweetly to his desire for more speed.

He caught up with the little red VW at a set of lights just before the turning off to her block. A modernized council high-rise that its old tenants would never have recognized, so luxurious had been its conversion to private apartments.

As she operated the device on her dash that opened the security gates to the underground car park, he used the one that he had duplicated, and swiftly followed her down the incline into the cool gloom of the deserted garage. He slotted the Cosworth into a space on the opposite side to where she put the Golf, and watched as she retrieved a Marks & Spencer carrier full of shopping, and her handbag, remotely locked the VW, and walked towards the lift.

He took a plastic half mask from the glove box and slid it on to his face and, snugly setting the elastic loop at the back over his head, got out of his car too, briefly catching sight of himself in the rear view mirror as he did so. The mask was brightly painted into a horrific grimace. Trace was pleased at the different aspect it gave to his looks.

He let the door of the car close to, but not latch, and silent on rubber soles he followed his target towards the lift so quietly that it wasn't until he whispered 'Hello, Penny,' that she realized she was not alone.

She frowned when he spoke her name, turned, saw the hideous countenance before her and opened her mouth to scream when he fired a canister of anaesthetic into her face.

'Welcome to the pleasure dome,' he said, as she dropped the carrier bag, spilling its contents of ready-cooked convenience meals, pasta sauce in dumpy glass jars, and plastic bottles of overpriced spring water on to the concrete floor of the garage. He caught her easily in his arms just before she joined her shopping.

3

He picked her up easily, and swiftly carried her to the Cosworth, where he manhandled the back door open and sat her on the seat, carefully fastening the seat belt to keep her upright, before going back and recovering her shopping, which he tossed in after her before slamming the door closed.

He climbed in behind the wheel, glanced round to see that she looked as if she had just fallen quietly asleep, smiled, removed the mask and threw it back into the glove compartment, started the car and drove out of the garage, back through the security gate towards Peckham.

The evening was turning to night when he arrived at the factory, and cars were turning on their headlights, but the air was still warm, and groups of drinkers were taking their leisure outside the pubs in the Old Kent Road.

Trace undid the padlock on the tall factory gates, pulled them open and drove the car into the courtyard. Only after he had closed the gates behind him could he relax and light one of the rare Marlboros he allowed himself.

The woman was still asleep in the back of the Ford, snoring gently, her head on one shoulder. A thin line of silver drool ran from the corner of her mouth to the lapel of her jacket.

Trace grimaced in disgust as he undid the seat belt and carried her into the building. People. He hated them.

Once inside, he lifted her on to the gynaecological examining table that stood in the middle of the cavernous ground floor of the factory on a vast sheet of industrial strength, black plastic sheeting. A big-screen TV hooked up to a stereo VCR with additional surroundsound speakers stood in front of her. He switched on both the TV and video machine, and one of the recordings of her lovemaking with a man she had picked up in a club one night began to play, their cries of enjoyment moving round from speaker to speaker.

He felt no desire as he stripped off her clothes, leaving only the brief, white lace panties that covered her sex.

He opened her legs wide and fastened her feet into the metal stirrups, stood back and admired his handiwork.

Good, he thought. Now for the optional extras, as ordered by the client.

He put on a pair of thick cotton gloves, picked up a pair of heavy-duty pliers from the workbench that ran down one side of the building, and found a roll of brand new, shiny barbed wire. He carefully cut off four lengths, and used them to fasten her hands and feet securely to the table, twisting the wire tightly with the pliers until the barbs cut into her soft flesh.

She moaned. He smiled, went to the bench, found another mask similar to the one he kept in the car, and put it on.

As he was fastening the last piece of wire, she opened her eyes.

She pulled her head up from the table, looked down the length of her semi-naked body, up at Trace, at the TV set, and opened her mouth to scream again.

'You'll be wasting your breath,' he said. 'No one can hear you, but it'll annoy me and I'll have to gag you.'

She licked her dry lips with a tongue coated in white, and said, in a voice very unlike the one he had heard on the tapes, 'You're hurting me.'

'No gain without pain,' he replied, and pushed one of the barbs deeper into the flesh of her right ankle.

Then she did scream. A long, drawn-out, high-pitched sound that echoed around the inside of the building. The crow that sat on the bumper of the Ford Cosworth outside cocked its head as the sound faintly leaked through the thick walls of the factory, but finally faded in the hum of the city.

4

Trace slapped her hard, and her head rocked from the force of the blow. She stopped screaming. 'Last chance,' he said.

She looked at the screen in front of her and said, 'Why?'

'Why not?'

She screamed again then, and Trace hit her for the second time. 'I warned you,' he said. He went and tore a strip of gaffer tape off a roll that also lay on the workbench and slapped it over her mouth, smoothing it down over her lips. 'Next time, maybe you'll listen.' He stepped back, looked at her, and nodded to himself. 'Stick around,' he said, as she rolled her head from side to side, her eyes wide with terror. 'Watch the movie. It's very good. I won't be long.'

He went outside to the car and rescued her carrier bag from where he'd thrown it, and returned to the factory, closing the thick door firmly behind him.

The crow, who had hopped into a dark corner of the factory at the sound of Trace's approach, watched his every move, before tucking its head beneath its wing and going to sleep.

Inside, Trace spread the food out on the bench. 'Good taste,' he said, as he picked up a box of tandoori chicken, a packet of nan bread, and a bottle of orange and raspberry juice. 'Time for supper, I think. Don't worry, I'll be back.' He mounted a flight of metal stairs that led up into the gloom above.

The first floor of the factory had been offices, and he had converted the largest one into a self-contained, luxury kitchen-cum-living room-cum-sleeping quarters. From the outside it still looked like the bulk of a dilapidated slum, but on the inside it had every comfort. There was only one jarring note. The walls were covered with framed, blown-up photos of napalm victims exposing their terrible burns, a Buddhist priest calmly setting fire to himself, the famous photo of a Vietnamese officer blowing the head off a suspected spy, the camera catching the precise moment when the bullet splashed brains and blood out in a spray. Photos from the Holocaust, taken at Belsen and Buchenwald as the allies invaded. And other more recent photographs from Rwanda, Bosnia, Grozny and Kobe.

Trace flipped on the lights, put the chicken and nan into the microwave and opened the juice and drank it straight from the bottle.

The food took only minutes to heat up, and he ate it from the containers, standing, looking through the filthy window across the city as the night deepened.

When his hunger was satisfied he went back downstairs to the woman, and flicked off the TV set.

She was still conscious, and the barbs cut deeper into her body as she flinched at his approach.

'You're probably wondering why I've brought you here,' he said. 'You probably imagine that I found you so attractive that I had to have you for my own.' He paused. 'Don't flatter yourself. You couldn't be more wrong. I don't give a damn about you as a person. Only as a way to earn money. In fact, I don't even know why I am doing this. You probably know better than me.

17

And maybe later, after you've had time to think, it'll come to you. I like to know the reason that I'm being employed. It gives it more of a personal touch.' He smiled down at her, and selected a scalpel from the selection that hung, gleaming, off a magnetized strip screwed to the wall. 'Are you sitting comfortably? Then we'll begin.'

Outside in the courtyard, the crow had woken up as it was joined by others. Dozens of others, who fluttered down silently to settle on the walls of the factory, on Trace's car, and on the roof of the building.

5

If the crows were interested in Trace's affairs that evening, they weren't the only ones. A number of people were thinking about him as he admired the way the blade of the scalpel caught the light. Most of them knew neither his name nor what he looked like. But all of them would have loved to know exactly where he was.

One in particular was less than a mile away, and could in fact have seen the factory where Trace conducted most of his grisly business if he had just turned his chair round 180 degrees and looked through the window behind him. Detective Chief Inspector Jack Dancer sat in his office at Peckham police station, stared at the pile of reports in front of him, and sighed. He was fifty years old, and could pass for forty. But he knew that his caffeine, alcohol, nicotine and cholesterol intake was high enough to send him down the slippery slope to heart attack city at any time. He ran his fingers through his dark hair, which was just beginning to fleck with grey, and lit another Silk Cut extra mild.

Fucking things, he thought, as he took the first drag. It'd be nice if you could even taste them. His sergeant, Steve Evans, came through the door carrying two cups of canteen tea.

'Evenin', Guv,' said Evans.

'Steve,' acknowledged Dancer as he took one of the cups. 'What's new?'

'Double shooting outside a pub on the Rye. Two spades. One dead, one in intensive care. Bit of a disagreement about a consignment of crack.'

'Will the one in hospital survive?'

'Hope not. Save us a fucking job. What about you?'

'Another body turned up. Down in Bermondsey. It's in a bad state.'

'Off our manor.'

'Yeah.' Dancer tapped the paperwork in front of him. 'But it's got a lot of similarities to these.'

'It's like stamp collecting to you, innit, Guv?' said Evans. 'You just love these weird cases. You can be too keen, you know.'

'Sure. But we're going to take a look anyway.'

'When?'

'As soon as we've drunk our tea. The body's waiting in the mortuary.'

'No rush then. It ain't going nowhere, is it?'

'No.'

'Any ID?'

'Not a thing.'

19

'Par for the course.'

'If it's the same firm.'

'What happened to this one?'

'Multiple injuries. Needles under the finger and toenails. Knuckles cracked with something. Pliers. Or maybe even a domestic nutcracker. Some teeth pulled. Various cuts and bruises.' He paused. 'Oh, and he'd been blinded.'

'Blinded?'

'Yeah. Eyes gouged out, and the sockets burnt. That's what killed him, the pathologist reckoned. The shock.'

Steve gulped. 'Charmin'.'

'That's what I thought.'

'There was another of them like that wasn't there?'

'Yeah.' Dancer dug through the files and pulled one out. 'Stanger. Alistair. Two months ago. Exactly the same.'

'You should put those files on to the computer, Guv,' said Evans. 'It's much neater.'

'I like paper,' said Dancer. 'Just call me old fashioned. I hate computers.'

'You're a Luddite, Guv. I bet you ain't even got a CD player either.'

'No, I haven't, as a matter of fact.' Dancer got to his feet, swallowed the last of his tea, and said. 'You coming?'

6

On the other side of the River Thames, someone else was thinking about Trace too. In fact, she never thought of anything else. She hadn't done for months. But at least she knew who he was. Her new friends had told her that. And where he was. She already knew what he did.

Her name was Mariella Cristobel Newman, née Koja, and she'd originally come from Mexico, but now she lived, if the solitary existence she led could be called living, in a house in a leafy square close to Harrods. It was a large house, much too big for one, but she knew that she could never leave it. The memories it held were too precious. And too monstrous.

That evening she was sitting in the lounge; a huge, high-ceilinged room on the first floor, which looked out over the square through vast French windows that opened on to a balcony. There were no lights on in the room, and the curtains moved sluggishly in a slight warm breeze that came from the west. Mariella sat in a brocade armchair and gazed at the faint square of sky she could see between the rooftops opposite, as the evening turned to night.

The room was silent except for the hum of traffic from the Cromwell and Old Brompton Roads, the occasional car that drove along the street outside, and the voices from passers by, amplified by the brickwork of the old houses on the square.

Mariella was used to the silence. She craved it like an

addict craves drugs. She sat holding a silver-framed photograph of a man and a small girl caught smiling together at a picnic in Hyde Park the previous summer. There were other pictures of the pair, together and separate, in frames all around the room on any available surface. Sometimes Mariella was in them too, sometimes not. And there were a few photographs of her alone. The photographs showed the development of all three of them from childhood. But there would be no more of her husband and baby, because they were both dead. The enormity of that truth suddenly brought tears to Mariella's eyes, and she clutched the photo she was holding so tightly that the glass almost cracked.

Eventually she placed the picture on the table next to her chair and got up. She walked through the dead air of the house, which had once been filled with the sound of her small family living their peaceful life together, to the kitchen, where she switched on one small light over the cooker, took a bottle of brandy from a cupboard, rinsed out one of the dozen or so dirty glasses that sat on the draining board, and poured herself a good measure.

She looked around. This room, of all the rooms, which had once been her pride and joy, where she had proudly cooked meals for herself and her family on the kind of equipment she would never have dreamed of owning as a girl in Mexico City, was now dusty and unkempt and littered with the detritus of takeaway food. She walked disconsolately back out into the hall and caught a glimpse of herself in the huge, gilt-framed mirror that hung on one wall.

In the splash of light from a street lamp outside, she grimaced as she saw that her once sleek, black hair was now streaked with grey, and had lost its style and become shaggy and matted. Her face, which her husband had thought so beautiful with its high cheekbones and olive skin, was drawn from crying, and her eyes had lost their sparkle. She was wearing a black sweater, dotted with dandruff on the shoulders, which she couldn't remember washing for months, and black leggings that were baggy at the knees.

What a mess, she thought, and raised the glass in a mock salute. Slowly she made her way upstairs to the attic conversion where she kept the icons she had brought from South America when she'd married Patrick Newman, and which were now her only solace. Her only comfort since her husband and daughter had been murdered in the very kitchen she had just left.

7

Trace spun the scalpel he was holding between his fingers, before turning back to the girl, who was so cruelly tied to the examining table.

'Have you had any thoughts about why you're here?' he asked as he tore the strip of tape off her mouth.

She licked her lips with a swollen tongue and swallowed hard, then shook her head.

'Aren't you interested?'

This time she nodded.

'So you should be. I would.'

She just looked at him.

'It's sort of like a guessing game,' said Trace. 'It'll help pass the time.'

Still nothing from the girl.

'Would you like a drink?' asked Trace. 'No champagne, I'm afraid, but I could manage some water.'

This time she nodded, and Trace put down the scalpel, went to a tap in one corner of the factory, drew some water into a clean glass and walked back to her. He supported her head with one hand and fed her the water slowly with the other. After a few sips she shook her head and he let it lie back on the table.

'Well?' he asked.

'No,' she replied. 'Is this some kind of a joke?'

'Your friends must have vicious senses of humour if you think that,' he replied. 'No. It's no joke. This is deadly serious.'

Tears suddenly filled the girl's eyes and began to run down her cheeks.

Trace looked at her and said, 'Save it. I'm not impressed. But I'm still interested in why someone's so interested in you. You're nothing, so it's not *what* you know.' He was almost talking to himself by then. 'It's that you've upset someone. That's obvious. Someone rich and powerful. Rich enough to be able to afford my services. Which don't come cheaply, let me tell you. You see sometimes I do my job to obtain specific information. It can be anything. A location. A name. A date. A business secret. That's what it usually is, but not you. With you, someone's paid me just to hurt you. Badly. Over a long period. And then spoil your pretty face and let you go.'

24

The girl made no sound or motion in reply, but just turned her head away and closed her eyes.

8

Before he began, Trace fastidiously talcum powdered his hands and pulled on a pair of thin, rubber surgeon's gloves. He didn't mind the feel of bodily fluids and blood. Enjoyed it even. But these days it paid to be careful when getting involved with strangers.

He looked down the length of her body. Once again he felt no desire as his eyes travelled up the length of her. Women didn't interest him. He couldn't remember the last time he'd had sex, only that it had been vaguely unsatisfying. The only real pleasure he'd experienced in that way was when he'd beaten a prostitute he'd bought, until her white body had turned black with bruises, and she'd bled from almost every orifice. No, there was no desire in his eyes, just curiosity to find out how much pain the young woman could stand.

He knew she was going to be a screamer, but he didn't mind that sort of noise when he was working. It was only before and after that it got on his nerves. From past experience he knew that however much racket she made inside the thick walls of the old factory, none of it ever reached the streets outside. And there was no human habitation for a quarter of a mile in any direction, the neighbouring buildings being boarded-up commercial lots, waiting for some financial wizard to come along, buy them up and wave a magic wand to convert them into a viable business proposition. Some fat chance in this part of London in this economic climate. She could yell herself hoarse, and no one would pay the slightest bit of attention. And besides, he wanted to tape the sounds she would make. Not only for his own personal satisfaction, but to supply to his client to prove that the job had been perfectly executed. So he went to the reel-to-reel tape machine that stood next to the TV, turned it on, tested the mike, and, once satisfied, allowed the reels to turn, a red light on the control panel indicating that recording was in progress.

He picked up the scalpel again and approached her. She whispered the single word 'no' before he began.

He started with her legs. Her right leg to be precise. He inserted the point of the blade under the skin on top of the bone in her calf and slid it up six inches or so. The blood leaked out and dripped down on to the table. She pulled her leg as far away as possible before the barbs on the wire tore through her flesh again, and she screamed.

Trace looked into her face. 'Hurts, doesn't it?' he said. 'Tell me why you're here and I'll make it hurt less.'

'I don't know,' she said, with a sob in her voice.

'Yes, you do. Now think.'

He saw her pucker up her face in concentration, then she said, 'There was this man.'

'Always a man,' he said, almost sadly.

'He worked for an affiliated company of ours in Germany.'

Germany, he mused to himself.

'He kept on asking me to go out with him. I had to go to Hamburg on a business trip, and met him there.'

'But you didn't do what he wanted?'

'No. I couldn't. He was repulsive. Fat. Old enough to be my father.'

'Perfect,' said Trace. 'Name?'

'Buchloz. Georg. Without an E.'

'Good old Georg,' said Trace. 'But why didn't you go out with him? You go with a lot of men. You don't seem over fussy.'

'How do you know?'

'I know everything about your sex life. I know the where, why and who. So why not him?'

'I'd heard about him from other women in the company he'd gone for.'

She really believed that by telling him so much he wouldn't continue with the job in hand.

He smiled. 'Go on,' he said.

'He's into some very strange stuff.'

He saw her look around the room as if this were normal. But of course, since he'd brought her to the factory, it was normal.

'Nazism. Rubber, leather. Whips. You know what I mean.' She went on.

Indeed I do, thought Trace.

'Pain. Lots of it.'

'So I imagine. That's why he hired me – if he hired me.'

'Weird sex,' she said. 'He had this metal chastity belt. It had a dildo built in, so you couldn't get the belt on without it going up you. Then you couldn't get it out without unlocking the belt. He made one woman wear it for nine hours straight.'

'Sexy,' Trace said.

She looked at him again, and licked her lips. 'Couldn't

we?' she said and bucked her hips. 'I can be good. Very good. And I've got a bit of money. You could tell him you did what he wanted—' She didn't finish her sentence.

'I know exactly what you're worth,' said Trace. 'Down to the last penny. And what your mother and father are worth too. And what you'd get if they both died tomorrow and made you sole beneficiary. Sorry. It's not enough. And besides, how long would I last in this business if I cheated on my clients? Not long, that's for sure. Now we've done enough talking. I think it's time to get to the interesting part.'

9

The blood on the top of her calf had already begun to clot, so Trace began to flay the skin on her thigh. He inserted the point of the scalpel under the epidermis and sliced the blade along about six inches as before. The metal was so sharp that it was easy. Rather like cutting butter. He pushed it through the thin layer of fat beneath the skin like a chef skinning a chicken. At the first contact of the steel she had started to scream again, and by the time he had finished the incision, a sharp smell of urine filled his nostrils as she voided her bladder.

He peeled the skin away from her flesh to an area of about six inches by four and tossed the flap of dead matter on to the plastic sheeting by his feet. He watched with satisfaction as the wound filled with blood and gently touched the bare tissue with his rubber-covered fingers, which made her scream louder.

'Let's make it even,' he said, and began to strip the skin from her other thigh. As the scalpel passed through the first layer, the girl passed out. Trace frowned and stopped. It was no fun when they were unconscious and unable to feel the gift of the exquisite pain he gave. His life's work. To him that feeling was better than any sex he'd ever had, and, naturally, he wanted to share it with someone who was awake.

He went over to the cold water tap and filled a small bucket to the brim. He walked back and threw the contents into the girl's face.

She came awake coughing and spluttering as the cold liquid filled her mouth and nasal passages. She shook drops from her hair, and he said, 'That's better. I didn't want you to miss the fun part.'

'You bastard,' she spat between clenched teeth. 'You said—'

'I said nothing,' Trace interrupted. 'You assumed. And it's always dangerous to assume. Didn't they teach you that at your smart office?'

She said nothing.

'Stupid little bitch,' Trace went on. 'I'm glad you came along. At least I can teach you some lessons before I'm finished with you. It's a shame you won't be able to use them in the outside world. You'd get along a lot better.'

The girl pursed her lips and spat at Trace.

'Fighting spirit,' he said. 'I like that.' And ground one of the barbs hard into her ankle.

'I hate you,' she screamed.

'Don't say that,' replied Trace. 'It tends to upset me.

29

You may hate me now, or think you do. But by the time I've finished with you, you'll love me. Most do. They tell me they love me and beg me to give them the ultimate release. The final orgasm. Death.' He winked at her and picked up the pliers he'd used to tighten the wire around her ankles and wrists. 'Manicure time, I think,' he said, and reached for her right hand.

The shriek that was wrenched from her mouth as he bent the nail of her ring finger back, ripping the nail from the tender skin beneath it, rang around the brick walls of the factory.

Blood dripped from her injured hand and pooled on the black plastic, and the heavy, cleated soles of Trace's shoes made tracks on its shiny surface as he paddled through the gore.

Through the agony from her injuries that had already aged her ten years in ten minutes, his victim looked up and whispered, 'You'll rot in hell for this.'

'I doubt it,' said Trace lightly, but before the long, hot summer had come to an end, he was to remember her words, and wonder if this was the day that it had all started.

10

Trace continued working on her right hand until there were five almond-shaped carmine nails floating in the blood on the floor. She kept passing out, and he kept reviving her. But he knew that he'd soon lose her from shock or loss of blood, if he wasn't careful. So, as the clock crept towards midnight he got the huge first-aid kit from the ambulance he'd stolen months before, and began to tend to her injuries.

He covered the skinless portions of her legs with emergency dressings and neatly bandaged her fingertips. She was only semi-conscious throughout, her colour was bad, and her breathing was shallow.

Not as tough as you thought, Trace said to himself, and gently undid the wire from her wrists and ankles before dressing the wounds the barbs had caused during her struggles.

He picked her up as if she were as light as a feather and carried her across the floor of the factory to one of the small rooms, which he had turned into a bedroom. Inside, it resembled a hospital ward, and Trace lay the girl on the narrow bed and covered her with a sheet and blanket before going back outside. He locked the door behind him, went upstairs to his quarters and fell into bed without looking outside, where the crows now resembled a heaving mass of jet that covered every square inch of the courtyard.

He awoke early. As the dawn spread its silvery fingers across the black roofs of south London, Trace rose from his bed, stretched and looked out across a courtyard which was now totally empty, and without any sign of the birds who had spent the night watching the factory.

He did his usual fifty press-ups, washed, shaved and cleaned his teeth as the kettle boiled for coffee, then donned his mask, and took the cup downstairs to see how the girl was.

31

She was awake and feverish, her face pale and drawn and her lips dry and caked with white foam. He pulled back the sheet and blanket to check her injuries. Her knickers were stained with urine and the birthmark on her hip was a livid red against the alabaster skin. Her legs seemed all right, but her hand was badly swollen, the knuckles like white dimples in the otherwise purple skin, and he thought that he could detect the first signs of gangrene.

She looked at him through dull eyes and said in a croaky voice, 'Can I go home soon?'

He nodded. 'Yes,' he said. 'Soon.'

'I need to use the loo.'

'Next door,' he said. 'Want any help?'

She tried to rise from the bed, but couldn't manage on her own, so Trace helped her to walk next door to one of the toilets that had served the workers in the factory.

She slumped down on the seat of the lavatory in the doorless cubicle and pulled her underpants down with her good hand. 'You don't have to watch,' she said. 'Or is that how you get off?'

Trace smiled. 'No, Penny,' he said. 'You'll find out how I get off later. Give me a shout if you need any more help.'

He stood outside the toilet in the cool air of the factory and watched as the rising sun shot shards of yellow through the filthy windows, and the atmosphere began to warm up.

A couple of minutes later she reappeared at the door of the lavatory, supporting herself on the jamb with her good arm.

'Feeling better?' asked Trace. 'Would you like some breakfast?'

'What kind of man are you?' she said. 'What kind of monster?'

'Just a man,' said Trace. 'Now, would you like some coffee?'

The girl nodded, and Trace said, 'I'm sorry. But I'll have to constrain you. Please come this way.'

He led her to a metal chair that had been bolted to the floor. Handcuffs hung from the arms and front legs.

'Sit down,' said Trace. 'I'll just cuff one hand. I don't think you'd get far. But I have to be sure.'

The girl fell on to the lightly padded seat, and Trace slid a cuff on to the wrist of the hand that was not swollen.

'I need a doctor,' said the girl. 'My hand. It's going bad.'

'Does it hurt?' asked Trace solicitously.

'Of course it fucking hurts, you idiot,' the girl shouted. 'You've ripped the bloody nails off. You've ruined it.' And she began to cry again.

Trace took his empty cup upstairs and filled it, and a clean one, then took them both downstairs. He found two croissants from the Marks and Spencer bag that he had brought in from the girl's car and said, 'Hungry?'

She shook her head.

'Please yourself,' he said, and took her the unsweetened black coffee. He put the cup on the floor and undid the cuff that held her arm. As he was kneeling by the chair fiddling with the lock, she lashed out with her right foot at his head.

He ducked away easily, and grabbed the hand from

which he had ripped her nails. The girl screamed once and fainted.

'Jesus,' he said. 'You just can't help some people,' and he kicked her cup of coffee across the floor.

He sipped from his own cup and chewed on one of the dry croissants until the girl moaned and opened her eyes. She nursed her bad hand against her breast, and Trace said, 'For that you don't get a drink.'

'Please,' she said, passing her tongue over her dry lips. 'I won't try anything again.'

'You won't get a chance. I'm sorry. I trusted you and you let me down. I don't forgive easily.'

'Please,' she said again.

Trace shook his head.

'People will be worried,' she said after a moment. 'They'll be looking for me.'

'Not here.'

'Just let me go. I won't tell anyone.' She was beginning to get hysterical, Trace could tell, and the one thing he couldn't stand was hysterical women.

'Shut up,' he said. 'I won't tell you again.'

She opened her mouth as if to speak, and he said, 'If you don't, I'll gag you.'

She closed her mouth again.

'Right,' said Trace. 'Back to the table.'

She looked over at the contraption of chrome and plastic with the stirrups rearing up obscenely from one end, and she cracked. She began to wail like a steam engine out of control. She tore at her hair and face with both her good and bad hands, until blood ran down her cheeks like scarlet tears.

Damn it, thought Trace. When they go crazy, they're no fun at all.

11

More quickly then, Trace began the last part of his job. First he took a syringe and filled it with anaesthetic and plunged it into the girl's arm. In her frenzy, she fought back hard, and the point of the needle broke off in the muscle. Trace punched her in the face, breaking her nose, and sending a stream of blood and snot out of both nostrils. He filled another syringe with the same mixture, and on the second attempt was able to pump the liquid into a vein. After a few minutes she began to calm down, and gradually became unconscious.

He picked her up from the chair and tossed her on to the examining table, not bothering to secure her arms and legs.

Roughly, he took her right arm and broke the elbow joint over his knee so that her hand flopped down at a strange, contorted angle. Then he repeated the process with her left.

Next, he picked up a ball-peen hammer and with almost delicate precision broke both her kneecaps, the splintered bone showing whitely through the torn skin. Then in a frenzy of violence he picked up the scalpel and began to slice lumps of live meat from her body, culminating in cutting a smile into her face with the point of the instrument. Finally he fried the hair from her head with a blow lamp, until her scalp blistered and popped with a smell like roasting pork, and hair fell from her head like clumps of blackened mattress stuffing.

During the ordeal she made not a sound.

He found a state-of-the-art Polaroid camera in the clutter on the bench and took close-up photographs of her injuries from every angle. Then made up another hypo of street-bought speed in a solution of water and adrenalin and pumped the load into the muscle closest to her heart and, as she came back to consciousness with a scream that would have curdled the blood of a Nazi concentration-camp guard, he filmed her awakening with a Sony mini-cam.

She came upright, her eyes the size of saucers. She tried to put her useless hands up to her face, where blood was dripping from the terrible wound he had inflicted on her mouth and was falling on to her bare breasts, and her scalp was peeling from her skull like ancient parchment. But she only screamed louder, as in their ruined state her hands wouldn't respond to the messages she was sending from her brain.

Trace smiled behind the viewfinder of the camera, as the girl thrashed about on the examination table, then tumbled on to the black plastic that covered the floor.

She flopped about like a slug under a rain of sea salt, and the blood from her wounds left a trail of brilliant red behind her. Trace watched her agonized movements with no emotion and filmed it all.

He looked at her broken body for several more minutes, then checked for vital signs. They were weak, but still discernible. Perfect, he thought, and went over and turned off the tape. Then he fired up the giant burner he had repaired. It didn't take long before it came up to full power and he opened the door to the furnace that roared inside, carefully dismantled the examination table and consigned it to the fire, closely followed by the scalpel and the hammer, the syringes, the girl's clothes and personal effects, the carrier bag and the remainder of her shopping, and anything else he could find that might tie him to her kidnap and torture. When he was satisfied he had got rid of everything, he slammed shut the door and, after donning gloves again, gently carried her out of the factory into the warm morning sunlight. He put her into the back of a Ford Transit panel van and locked the rear doors.

He opened the factory gate, looked carefully up and down the deserted street, then walked back to the truck, got in and started it with a roar from its powerful diesel engine, drove past the Cosworth, through the gate, got out of the Transit, leaving it idling at the kerb, secured the gate behind him, and after getting back into the cab, turned the vehicle in the direction of the river.

12

At about the same time as the flock of crows had begun to gather outside the factory in Peckham, DCI Dancer and DS Evans were admitted to the south London mortuary in Waterloo.

The body they were looking at was laid out on an aluminium pathology table, slightly angled downwards so that any blood and bodily fluids could roll down the grooves in the metal to the drain at the lower end.

The cadaver was of a man aged about forty, in the early stages of decomposition, and had already been cut open from throat to groin for examination. The top of the skull had been cut off and the brain removed.

The body's hands were disfigured where the knuckles had been cracked, and the digits lay at strange angles. There was severe discoloration of the fingernails, more than would normally have occurred after death, from where needles had been forced down into the soft skin beneath them. There were ligature marks on the wrists and ankles. The mouth of the dead man was propped wide to show where a number of teeth had been cleanly removed, and a number of others smashed by some heavy implement, as someone had tried to remove them too. But most horrific was the fact that the corpse stared upwards at the high ceiling through eyeless sockets that were black and blistered by fire.

The smell coming from the body was foul, and Dancer covered his mouth with a handkerchief,

Evans, who fancied himself the tougher of the pair, but was not prepared for the absence of eyeballs in the body, looked at his guv'nor and said, 'Jesus, Boss. Do we have to?'

'Just take a look,' said Dancer. 'I'm not asking you to sleep with him. And don't call me Boss.'

The pathology assistant, who was sitting with one buttock hunkered up on a laboratory bench close by, eating a Big Mac, and flicking through the latest copy of *Penthouse*, jumped down from his seat and joined them, still holding the hamburger in his hand. The smell of cooked meat almost made Evans retch, despite himself.

'Must you?' the younger policeman asked.

'Busy day,' said the pathology assistant. 'Non stop. Go, go, go. Stiffs coming out of our ears. No time for a relaxing meal down at the local chinky. Not like you blokes, always stopping for refreshment breaks.'

'I wish,' said Dancer. 'Can we get out of here?'

'I thought you wanted to view the body,' said the pathology assistant.

'I think we've seen enough,' said Dancer. 'Let's talk outside.'

'Fine,' said the pathology assistant, then to Evans, 'Want a bite?' He proffered the half-eaten snack in Evans' direction, grinning as the younger policeman blanched.

'Leave him alone,' said Dancer. 'We're short staffed enough as it is.'

All three of them went outside into the corridor, and Dancer said to the pathology assistant, 'Your boss around?'

'What, him? No, he's at home watching TV. Left me to mind the store and clean up the mess.'

'How exactly did that man in there die?'

'It's all in the report,' replied the pathology assistant, producing a thin sheaf of paper from the pocket of his lab coat and giving it to Dancer. 'Shock, probably. But he's pretty messed up, as you can see. You don't have your eyes gouged out and expect to collect your pension.'

'And he was found dumped in Bermondsey?'

'Dock Head to be precise. The local police have got all the details.'

'All wrapped up in black plastic sheeting.'

'Just like a Christmas present. Forensics have taken it down for examination.

'Right, thanks,' said Dancer. 'I'll get the full SP from them.'

'There must've been a run on that sheeting lately,' said the pathology assistant as he swallowed the last of his supper. 'That's the fourth one we've had in like that this year.'

'And there's been a couple of others north of the river,' said Dancer. 'Seems like we're looking for a serial killer. A particularly nasty one at that.'

'Then good luck,' said the pathology assistant. 'I think you're going to need it.'

'Cheers,' said Dancer, then to Evans, 'Come on, son, you look like you could use some fresh air.'

As they left, a crow on the weather vane cocked its head and cawed softly to itself.

13

Once they were in the car, Dancer said, 'Just the same as Stanger. I told you.'

'Any ID on this bloke?'

'Not so far. His prints and description are going through the system right now.'

'Whoever's doing it's a weird cunt.'

'Too true.'

'We can assume it's the same person?'

'I think so. The black plastic is the link.'

'And we can find no connection apart from that?'

'Apart from the fact they they're all well off. At least relatively.'

'And none of those who've survived will talk?'

'Those that can, won't. And those that can't, well, you've seen one or two of them.'

'It's bad news, Boss.'

'I told you, don't call me Boss. We're not in some bloody TV series.'

'Sometimes I wish we were. At least we'd be sure of solving all our cases in less than an hour.'

'You're quite a philosopher, Evans, you know that?' said Dancer, and started the engine.

As he did so, with a clatter of talons on metal, the crow that had been sitting on the weather vane landed on the bonnet of the car.

Both Dancer and Evans jumped as the bird pecked viciously at the windscreen, as if intent on smashing through and devouring the occupants.

'Jesus Christ,' said Evans. 'What the fuck . . .'

'Damn thing's gone insane,' said Dancer, and switched on the windscreen wipers at double speed. The bird recoiled and skittered crazily on the bonnet for a second before taking flight and vanishing into the darkness.

'What a world,' said Dancer as he switched off the wipers. 'Even the wildlife's gone fucking mad.'

14

When they got back to their office, Dancer and Evans collected two cups of tea and went over their case notes together.

'So far we've had three walking wounded found wandering around London, and four bodies discovered wrapped in black plastic and dumped close to the river this year,' said Dancer, lighting a cigarette. 'The dead ones showing the same signs of being tortured as the living, if you can call the state they're in living. Personally I'd rather be brown bread any time. The sheeting's industrial-grade plastic that can be bought from any one of a thousand outlets up and down the country. There's no way of identifying the particular pieces we have, and there's no trace of prints or any blood for DNA purposes, apart from the victims themselves.'

He got up and walked over to the window.

'The dead bodies are of both sexes and range in age from early twenties to late sixties, and we can find no connection except for the fact, as I told you before, that they're all pretty well heeled. They were all naked when they were found, and no one's turned up any of their clothes or personal effects since. The live ones were naked too, and ditto on the effects. All in the same age range. Plus, I've been doing a bit of research into some other unsolved murders and I've come up with a couple of interesting ones.' He tapped a thin pile of paper sitting on the corner of his desk. 'There have been two other similar torture/murders where the victims have been found at their homes or places of business. I want you to have a look at these, Steve, and tell me what you think. One in particular was very nasty. A pair of bodies found in a house in Kensington, last winter. February fourth. A father and daughter. The father had been pretty badly worked over, and it looks like the daughter interrupted the fun. The killer sliced her up as well. It was a botched job. I think it's the same man who's done all the others. And this was his first mistake. I've talked to the officer in charge of the case. He hasn't got a clue. So tomorrow we're going round to try and interview the wife. She found the bodies, and took it very badly. Which is only to be expected. She's become something of a recluse since it happened. She's got money. You don't live where they did unless you have. But we've got to go carefully. Her doctor's very worried about her. He thinks it wouldn't take much to send her over the top, so we'll take a female officer with us.'

'I'm supposed to be off tomorrow, sir,' said Evans.

'Got a bit of gardening to do?'

'No. I thought I'd catch up on some sleep, and reintroduce myself to my wife. I haven't seen too much of her lately.'

'Do that another time,' said Dancer. 'This bloke is beginning to get to me, and I want him caught. He's teasing us, the bastard. There's been a lot of talk about a certain party who'll torture a victim of your choice for a fee. A large fee. And I don't like it. Gives everyone else ideas. This bastard needs to be convicted, and we're just the people to do it.'

'Who told you all that?' said Evans. 'Sounds like a lot of old bollocks to me.'

'That little shit Mallory. Your snout, originally. You told me he never lied when you passed him over.'

'OK,' said Evans with a sigh. 'What time?'

'Midday.'

'Just time for me to go home, have a shower, get changed and ignore my bed and missus again.'

'And you'll be bright and early for our shift tomorrow night. Come on Steve, own up. You know you love it.'

'Well, it's not the money, Guv'nor. That's for sure.'

Unaware that she was being discussed, Mariella Newman was sitting in the attic of the house in Knightsbridge. The room was dimly illuminated by candles, and the light barely reached the corners, which were wreathed in shadows. She was no longer alone. Perched on the backs of chairs, on the edges of the shelves that lined the attic, and on the floor, were maybe a hundred crows. They had come in through the dormer window which was wide open and showed the crescent of the moon. Mariella sat on the edge of an old, overstuffed sofa. Next to her was the figure of a man, dressed in a dusty black coat and stovepipe trousers over a clean white shirt and black bootlace tie. His boots were as black and shiny as the wings of the crows, as was his full head of long, straight hair. In her hands Mariella was holding a crystal ball that caught the light from the candles and the reflection of the moon and threw it round the room where it glittered off the watchful eyes of the birds, and the man who was there.

'Is there any news?' asked Mariella in the guttural tongue of her native land.

'Plenty,' the man replied in the same language. His voice was just a rasp.

'Tell me.'

'His name is Trace. Matthew Trace.'

'And you know where he is?'

The man nodded.

'And what can you do?'

'That is up to you.'

'Kill him,' she said, and as one, the crows moved their feathers with a sinister rustle at her words.

'It is not yet his time,' said the man.

'Yes, it is,' insisted Mariella. 'I want it to be his time.'

'You are strong, mistress,' said the man. 'But not strong enough.'

'Then who is stronger? I demand to know.'

'There is only one. I do not speak His name.'

Mariella smiled mirthlessly. 'I do,' she said.

'It is not wise.'

'I don't care for wisdom,' said the woman. 'What good has wisdom done me?'

The man did not reply.

'I demand an audience with The One,' said Mariella Newman.

The crows moved fitfully again, and one or two cawed softly, until her sharp gaze silenced them.

'He does not meet with just anybody.'

'You dare to call me *anybody*,' said the woman. As light jumped inside the crystal ball she was holding, the man moved back against the cushion he was leaning on. 'I do not care to be referred to as such by you.'

The man put up a placating hand. 'Forgive me, mistress,' he said. 'But there are other plans for Trace. The

One is angry with him. He moves into forbidden areas, where mortals should not venture.'

'*Angry*,' screamed the woman, and the birds moved as far away from her as they could go. 'I, too, am angry. I travelled thousands of miles from my native land to this cold and thankless country. I left my powers behind on His bidding. I agreed not to practise what I learnt as a child in exchange for peace. But what kind of peace did I find? A few short years of happiness, and then my husband and daughter were destroyed. If I had been given some warning I could have prevented it, but no. I was left alone. And if I had not brought a few artefacts with me, I would never have been able to summon you back. Did you have a good holiday in my absence?'

'We were waiting for your call.'

'But in the meantime you seem to have forgotten who I am.'

'No, mistress.'

'Then arrange a meeting.'

'Yes, mistress.'

'Now get out of my sight. I have a feeling I need my rest. Someone is coming to see me tomorrow, and I'll need all my wits about me.'

'Yes, mistress.'

'Then go, and don't let me see your face until you have some better tidings.' With that, Mariella Newman rose from her seat and left the room, still carrying the crystal ball.

Within a few minutes the attic was empty, as if no one had been in there for years.

15

Friday morning, as the sun was almost at its zenith, two vehicles were driving up the Old Kent Road in a northerly direction. They were only a couple of car lengths apart, but neither the occupant of the Transit van nor the three officers in the unmarked police car following it were aware of each other, although already their destinies were implacably entwined.

Above flew two crows, buoyed up by the heat from the fumes of the traffic heading to and from central London.

Trace, at the wheel of the truck with the girl in the back, whistled to himself as he drove. He was running a map of the area through his mind before deciding where to dump her.

Two cars back, Dancer and Evans were explaining their mission to the young plain-clothes officer accompanying them to the interview with Mariella Newman.

'We've tried phoning the house this morning, but there's no answer,' said Dancer, half turning in his seat so that he could look at the face of WPC Jane King sitting in the back. 'But that doesn't necessarily mean she's not at home. Apparently she doesn't answer the phone much these days. So we might be on a wild-goose chase. She's had a terrible time of it, what with finding the bodies of her husband and daughter, and being a stranger in this country. But apparently she refuses to move from the place. It's not healthy for the woman, but she won't listen to anyone. She says she has to be where they were all happy together.'

'Morbid, I call it,' said Evans, as he swapped lanes and pulled up next to the anonymous-looking panel truck.

Evans glanced past Dancer at the driver of the truck, who returned his look for a second from behind the dense lenses of his Porsche sunglasses before indicating a right turn at the Bricklayers Arms roundabout, leaving Evans and his companions to head straight on to the Elephant & Castle. High above them, one crow peeled off and followed Trace, the other kept up with the police car.

Evans concentrated on negotiating his car through the heavy pre-lunchtime traffic.

'Call it what you like,' said Dancer to his sergeant. 'That's the way she's playing it, and who are we to argue?'

'And you want me to lend the feminine touch, is that it, Guv?' asked Jane King.

'Spot on,' said Dancer. 'Perhaps she'll tell you things she wouldn't tell us.'

'And perhaps she won't,' said Jane King under her breath, who, although she was young, was also, after a year of plain-clothes work in a run down part of south London, pretty cynical too.

'It's worth a try,' said Dancer.

As the police car crossed Vauxhall Bridge en route to Kensington, Matt Trace steered the Transit into an alleyway that had been formed between two new office developments just west of Blackfriars Bridge.

He climbed out, stretched and looked around. The

48

alley was deserted. He looked up at the featureless walls that loomed above him, and all he saw was a single crow on the edge of the roofline. Trace walked towards the end of the alley which looked out across the river, squinted into the sun and nodded to himself. The tide was going out. Beneath him lay a demolished jetty with a thin frill of filthy mud exposed between the pilings, which jutted into the air like rotten teeth in a mouthful of diseased gums. The mud was beginning to steam in the heat, and it stunk like a disinterred corpse.

Very fitting, thought the Torturer, and went back for the body.

She was still alive, but barely, as he manhandled her naked body out of the back of the truck, slung it over his shoulder, walked down to the river's edge, took one more look up and down the bank, and dropped her on to the filthy beach below. She landed with a soggy splash, and without looking back Trace returned to his truck, started it up, reversed it out of the alley, and turned back in the direction of Peckham.

Once there, he checked the burner, which by then had destroyed the evidence he had dumped inside it, then collected the Ford Cosworth and headed towards Greenwich, and one of the secret lairs that he called home.

The huge black bird followed him every inch of the way.

Evans parked the police car legally on a meter just around the corner from Mariella Newman's house, and after feeding some coins into the slot, and meticulously putting the amount in his notebook to claim back later, he, Dancer and King walked round to her front door, under the eye of the crow that was perched on the top of a plane tree.

Dancer rang the bell, then banged hard with a brass knocker that was shaped like a fish.

There was no answer, and no sound from within, so he repeated the exercise.

'Sod,' he said.

'There is someone in,' said Jane King, who had moved back down the wide flight of stone steps, and stood on the pavement looking up at the front of the house, which seemed to glare balefully back through the eyes of its windows. 'I saw the curtains move on the top floor.'

Dancer nodded and attacked the door again. After some minutes' wait he saw movement behind the translucent glass panels at the top of the door, and a few seconds later it opened on a chain.

'Mrs Newman?' he asked of the one dark eye that peered out. It was set in a pale-skinned face, and topped with unruly black hair that was going grey.

The face nodded.

Dancer produced his warrant card. 'Detective Chief Inspector Jack Dancer, Metropolitan Police. These are my colleagues, Sergeant Evans and DC King. I'm sorry to call without an appointment, but I've tried several times to contact you by telephone.'

'I know,' said the woman, still behind the door.

'How do you know?' asked Dancer, somewhat surprised by her words.

'I knew that you, or someone like you, would call.'

Dancer chose to ignore the road they were going

down, and said, 'I wonder if we could come in and speak to you?'

'About my husband and daughter?'

'Amongst other things.'

Dancer thought he saw a smile cross her face. It was gone in an instant, and he hoped that he'd imagined it, as it was far from pleasant.

'Of course,' she said as she stood back, disengaged the chain and opened the door fully. 'I'm afraid I've rather neglected the place lately, but come in anyway.'

16

The hall which they entered was dark and dusty, and cobwebs hung from the shadowy corners. Dancer and the others saw what she'd meant by neglect. But then, she no longer had a family to be houseproud for.

'Come upstairs,' the woman said to them. 'I more or less camp out in the kitchen these days.'

The room was still dirty, the fast-food containers still littered every surface, and the dishes sat in the sink giving off an odour of decay and neglect.

'Sit, if you can find anywhere,' said Mariella Newman carelessly. 'Would anyone like coffee? I've no milk or sugar, I'm afraid.'

All three police officers declined, and cleared spaces for themselves on three hard kitchen chairs. Mariella stood by the sink in front of the window so that she was not much more than a silhouette to the trio.

'I'm sorry to go over old events,' said Dancer. 'And open old wounds—'

'My wounds are still very much wide open, officer,' replied Mariella Newman. 'Nothing you can say or do will alter that.'

'Except catch the man who killed your family,' said Dancer.

'Even that cannot bring them back,' retorted the woman. 'Now, please, ask your questions and leave.'

Not at all fazed by her attitude, Dancer continued. 'I didn't work on the case myself,' he explained. 'But certain similarities between it and other cases I *am* currently investigating have come to light.'

'Such as?'

'I'm sorry, Mrs Newman, but we understand that your husband was tortured before he was killed.'

'*Understand*,' the woman said, coming bolt upright. 'You *understand*. I very much doubt that, officer. Only if you'd seen him as I found him would you even begin to understand.'

Seeing her obvious distress, Jane King came to her feet and said, 'Would *you* like a drink, Mrs Newman?'

The older woman looked at the younger and said, 'Yes, I would. Brandy. It's in the cupboard there.'

Without turning a hair at her request, Jane King fetched the bottle, washed a glass and filled it a quarter full. 'Is there anywhere more comfortable to sit?'

'The living room downstairs,' volunteered Mariella Newman.

'Then why don't the two of us go and do just that. We can have a talk if you like, or not. Just see how you feel.' She looked at Dancer and Evans and said, 'I'm sure my

52

two colleagues could do with a pint and lunch, and I think I saw a pub on the corner when we came in.'

Dancer took the hint. 'Good idea,' he said. 'Will you join us later, Jane?'

'As soon as Mrs Newman is feeling better,' replied the WPC, her cynicism forgotten as she gently led the widow out of the room.

The two men followed them down a flight of stairs, then continued to the ground floor where they let themselves out on to the street.

'Rather her than me,' said Evans as soon as they got outside, and Dancer nodded in agreement.

Meanwhile, Jane King and Mariella Newman had both found seats inside the living room, and Mariella was sipping from her brandy as the policewoman looked at the photographs that filled the room.

'You had a lovely family,' she said after a moment.

'*Had* is right,' said Mariella.

'I'm sorry. Whatever you say in circumstances like this sounds wrong.'

'Don't blame yourself,' said the older woman in a kinder tone. 'I know it cannot be easy for you.'

'It isn't. It's a man's world in the police force. I have to be tougher than them to get on. Or at least pretend that I am.'

'So. What did you want to know?' asked Mariella Newman.

Already briefed by Dancer on the drive up, Jane King said, 'Have you any idea why your husband was a victim?'

'None.'

'He worked for a merchant bank, I believe.'

'He was a director. He had a very good job for a man who was relatively so young.'

'You speak good English, Mrs Newman. But I believe you come from Mexico originally.'

'Correct. But English is the second language there. And I was born very poor. I wanted a good job, so I had to speak English as well as I could. Then I met Patrick. I was working at the Mexico City branch of the bank. He came in as a troubleshooter. We fell in love, got married, and when he was transferred back to London, naturally I came. I wasn't working then, I'd already had Nadia.'

At the mention of her daughter's name, her face crumpled, and she gripped the glass hard between her two hands to hold it steady as she took a long swallow of liquor.

'I'm so sorry,' said Jane King. 'Can you tell me what happened that day?'

'I've already told it a thousand times.'

'I realize that. But you never know. I'm sure you've gone over it a million times in your mind since, and telling me just might shake something new loose.'

'Very well,' said Mariella Newman. And she began.

'It was a Wednesday,' she said. 'I'll never forget it until the day I die. I had arranged to visit my mother-in-law. She lives down in Brighton. She's never got over the shock of Patrick and Nadia's death. She's in a home now. Another life ruined. Nadia was at grade school. Junior school you call it here. We had her in a private lycée in Knightsbridge. But she caught a cold. It was February. This country is so cold in the winter. I never got used to it, and now I never will. Patrick was working on a new project. His office was in Cheapside. The City.

54

But he'd brought his papers and computer disks home so that he could work in the privacy of his study here. It was very confidential. A new share flotation or something. He wouldn't even discuss it with me. I wanted to stay at home with Nadia, but he insisted that he could take care of her ...' She paused and wiped her eyes at the remembered pain. 'He really loved his little girl. And me. And I loved them too. So I went to Brighton. I had lunch in a restaurant in The Lanes with his mother, then caught a train back at four o'clock. The train was delayed, I had trouble getting a taxi and the traffic was awful, so that it was almost six thirty before I got back here. It was full dark and every light in the house seemed to be on.'

She paused then, for a long time, and Jane King reached over to touch her hand, but she pulled away.

'I let myself in. I had a present for Nadia that I'd bought in an antique shop. It's over there.' She pointed in the direction of a tiny silver horse and rider that sat next to one of the pictures of her late husband and child. 'She loved horses. She could ride well. She wanted one of her own, but living like we did in the city ...' Another pause. 'But one day we were going to move. Anyway, I walked in and called their names. There was no answer. I went up to Patrick's study first. It was on this floor. Next door, in fact. Nadia's bedroom was on the third floor, next to ours, under the attic. He had been' – she took another hit from her glass – 'mutilated. Terribly. Tied up and tortured. His face was like a mask. A rictus is the word. I looked it up. I hate to neglect my vocabulary.' Tears were pouring from her eyes, and Jane King gave her a stack of tissues from her handbag.

'He had been bound and gagged, but he'd bitten through the gag before he died. His tongue was sticking out. It was blue. So were his . . . his genitalia. Whoever killed him had wrapped a metal coat hanger around them. It cut off the circulation. It was horrible. Then he'd attached an electric battery to them. The hair was all burnt off. His arms and legs were broken. The bones were sticking out like splinters of wood. The soles of his feet had been burnt until the flesh melted and dripped on to the floor. The smell of burning flesh from them and his groin was terrible. I can still smell it sometimes when I go into the room. And his eyes had been stapled open. That was the worst I think. His eyes had been stapled open so that he had to watch himself being mutilated, and our little girl murdered.'

Jane King swallowed hard. She'd seen some shit since she'd been a copper, but this was beyond her worst nightmares.

'What happened to your daughter?' She had to ask, although she'd read the reports that Dancer had brought with him. But for some perverse reason she had to hear it first hand.

'She must have heard something and come downstairs,' said Mariella Newman. 'She was still in her nightdress. I bought it for her for Christmas from a shop in Fulham. It was so pretty. Pale blue with little teddy bears embroidered round the neckline. She must have surprised whoever was doing those horrible things to Patrick. He obviously thought she was at school. Can you imagine what she thought? She was only eight for God's sake.' Mariella crossed herself. 'He stabbed her more than twenty times. Her nightdress was ruined.'

The real tears came then, in floods that washed down Mariella Newman's face like a waterfall of grief.

Jane King said, 'I'm truly sorry to remind you of that day.'

'Don't be sorry,' replied Mariella sharply. 'I need to be reminded. I need to remember that day until the day that I too die, and join my husband and daughter in the afterlife. That is why I stay here in this house and do not go home to my family in Mexico. Every minute I think of the man who did this dreadful thing, and pray that one day soon he will receive his just rewards for the horror he perpetrated.'

'And you have no idea—'

'No,' lied Mariella Newman firmly. 'When I got back he was gone. He left no clues. You must know that.'

'I do. But we believe he is responsible for many other similar murders.'

'I know. The other policeman said that too. The one who investigated last winter. He was a very nice man, but I knew he wouldn't be able to do anything. Such evil can only be repaid by more evil.'

'I hope you don't really believe that,' said Jane King. 'We'll catch him, I promise.'

'Please do not make any promises you cannot keep,' said Mariella Newman.

'And there is nothing else you can think of that might help us in our inquiries?'

'No,' lied Mariella Newman again, and the flock of crows that had gathered on the roof of the house stamped their taloned feet on the slates as she told her lies.

'Then I'd better find my boss,' said Jane King. 'He'll

be wondering what's become of me. And once more, I'm sorry.' But even as she spoke she realized the emptiness of her words. 'Please take my card. And any time you need to talk, please call me.'

'Thank you,' said Mariella Newman, accepting the piece of white pasteboard that Jane King took from her handbag.

The older woman showed the younger to the door, then moved to the ground floor front room and watched as the attractive blonde walked towards the pub where her superiors were waiting. As she watched, Mariella Newman scowled, crushed the card in her fist and said to herself, 'You'll never catch him, you stupid girl. You and your whole police force will never get near him. But I will. I and my friends will. Take my word. We will have our own revenge, without recourse to your law.' She turned, dropped the card to the dusty carpet beneath her feet, and as she left the room kicked it into a dark corner where it lay ignored for the rest of the summer.

17

Jane King was pale and shaky by the time she found Dancer and Evans sitting in the shady garden of the pub, half-finished pints and the remains of a sandwich lunch in front of them. It was unusual for anything to ruffle her cool exterior, and she wasn't happy.

'It's all right for some,' she said harshly as she walked up to them.

'You look like you need a brandy,' said Dancer.

'No more brandy,' replied King. 'I can still smell it from that horrible house. I'll have a G and T. A large one.'

'Anything to eat?'

'God, no. Just a drink.'

'Steve,' said Dancer, and Evans got to his feet and went inside to the bar.

'Rough?' asked Dancer.

'The worst,' said King. She sat in Evans' vacated chair and took one of Dancer's cigarettes from the open pack in front of him.

He lit it for her, she inhaled deeply and let out twin plumes of grey smoke from her nostrils.

'I needed that,' she said. 'That place gave me the creeps, and I've been to some bad ones, but that place stunk of ... evil. Yes that's it. Evil. She talked about that too.'

'What did she say?'

'That only a greater evil could deal with anyone who did what that person did to her family.'

'I hope you put her right.'

'I tried to. But I don't think I succeeded.'

'Did she come up with anything new?'

'Not a thing. It was a complete waste of time.'

'No such animal in this job, love. Take my word. You never know when the smallest sliver of information can grow to giant proportions, maybe months, maybe years after the event.'

Then Evans came back with Jane King's drink and refills for the two men.

'So, what's up?' he asked, casting another appreciative glance at Jane King's thighs.

'Nothing,' she said, taking a long swig of her drink. 'Nothing at all.'

'So what did she say?' the younger man asked.

'Just that,' replied Jane King. 'Nothing. Nothing at all. Now can we leave it, please.'

Evans looked at Dancer, who shook his head slightly, and Evans wisely decided to leave it. After a while they finished their drinks, rescued the car, and drove back to Peckham.

18

Trace's Greenwich bolt hole was a detached house at the end of a cul-de-sac so close to the river that he could hear the mournful sound of foghorns on misty mornings, and smell the dirty tang of the water when the wind came from the north.

He drove the Cosworth up the almost-rural lane to the house, which stood beetle-browed behind a high fence and thorny hedge. Pressing a button on the remote control mounted on the car's dash, he waited whilst the gate and garage doors opened in tandem, then drove through before the fifteen-second timer on the gate motor closed the gate behind him. He put the car inside the double garage next to an anonymous-looking, beaten-up BMW 5-series coupé, got out and closed the garage door with the switch on the wall.

The ceiling light had come on automatically as the gate closed, and using it for illumination, he unlocked the door that led from the garage to the huge kitchen which took up most of the ground floor of the large house.

He opened the fridge, looked inside, made a face, shrugged, then brought out a bottle of mineral water, unscrewed the cap and swallowed half straight from the neck.

Then he went and checked his answering machine which stood in the drawing room. The telephone number at the house, like the ones at his other hideouts, was monitored through two switching boxes located at accommodation addresses as far apart as Bristol and Leeds. These had an automatic kill switch that would turn the inside of the boxes to molten plastic and melted wire if they were ever disturbed and, with any luck take the hands off the person who had done the interfering. It was as close to a foolproof way for Trace to protect the identity of his illegally procured number which, if it were ever traced, belonged to the convent of an order of nuns located in Harrow-on-the-Hill, who had taken an unbreakable vow of silence. Trace had often wondered why they bothered to have a phone at all, because not once in the year he had used it, had an actual call come through for the nunnery.

The red light on the answering machine was blinking, and he hit the message button.

'*You're wanted,*' said a voice that Trace recognized as one of his many contacts, although the pair had never met face-to-face, and were never likely to. '*Phone yellow-ten at seven p.m. every day. This is Wednesday.*

61

They'll wait six.' No names were ever used over public land lines.

The voice had said it was Wednesday, which meant the call had come on Monday. *They'll wait six* meant that whoever needed his unique talents would wait for an answer until Sunday. *Call yellow-ten at seven p.m.*, meant call the contact at his place of business at seven p.m. minus ten hours, any day up until then. Nine a.m. It was now Friday afternoon, so he could call tomorrow, Saturday morning.

Good, thought Trace. I could use another gig, and he checked the machine for further calls, of which there were none, and then went back to the fridge for another bottle of water.

19

That same evening Mariella Newman talked again to the Crow Man and his avifauna companions in the attic of the house in Kensington.

'We must hasten in our task,' she said. 'They came today as I said they would.'

'We are aware of that, mistress. They were followed.'

'Trace is out of control,' she said. 'I'm afraid that by some stroke of luck the police may apprehend him before we do.'

'That is impossible, mistress,' said the Crow Man. 'He will not allow it.'

'It could happen by accident. The Torturer is getting careless. His luck has been too good.'

'And so it will continue to be,' said the Crow Man. 'At least until he has fulfilled one particular task.'

'When I summoned you,' said Mariella Newman, 'it was to destroy him, not to keep him alive and well. You should obey me, and do as I want.' She was almost petulant.

'We will, mistress,' said the Crow Man. 'But there are greater authorities than yours that we must answer to. As soon as his task is complete, we will do your bidding.'

'Why can only Trace do it?'

'Because he will. It is ordained. He told us.'

'Damn Him,' said Mariella Newman. 'Damn them both.'

'Hush, mistress,' said the Crow Man. 'It is not wise to speak of the Great Beast thus. He has spies everywhere.'

Mariella dismissed him and his friends with a contemptuous wave of her hand and went back downstairs to the living room and her photographs and brandy bottle.

Trace spent a peaceful night in the huge bed in the master bedroom of the house in Greenwich, which had never known more than a single occupant, was up early, and breakfasted before eight.

At nine on the dot he rang his contact on the special number that he, and he alone used.

'Yellow,' he said when the phone was picked up after one ring.

'Mercantile Union building. Three, three.' And Yellow put down the phone.

The call meant that the key to a coin-operated locker was taped under the cistern of the third cubicle from the door in the gents on the third floor of the Mercantile Union building in London Wall. The lockers were situated in the members-only section of the health club that operated out of the basement of the building.

Getting in would be easy for Trace. Even on a Saturday morning when the building was closed.

He stopped off in Peckham, changed into a pair of faded blue jeans, a dark blue polo shirt, a many-pocketed nylon waistcoat, and battered work boots. From a filing cabinet in the tiny office he kept on the top floor of the factory he selected a photo ID card in a plastic case and slung it round his neck by the cord that slotted through the hole in one corner. From the garage he picked up a leather tool belt, a radio receiver-transmitter complete with a fresh set of batteries, and a yellow hard hat, and climbed into the Cosworth. He put on his sunglasses, operated the button on the dash again and drove through the front gate and back to the main road towards the City of London.

He parked the Ford in a side turning just off London Wall and was at the Mercantile Union building by ten past ten, the hard hat on his head. The glass doors were locked, and he peered through and saw a uniformed commissionaire sitting at a desk behind a bank of video screens. There was a bell next to the door. Trace pushed the button.

He saw the commissionaire look up, frown and shake his head. Trace grinned in a friendly way and held up his pass.

From where he was sitting the man had no chance of

seeing what the pass designated, so he climbed to his feet and made his way to the door, where Trace pressed the plastic against the glass. It showed that Trace, or at least a certain Charles Andrews with Trace's photo next to the name, worked for the City of London Department of Sanitation, and the commissionaire keyed open the door. 'Sorry to bother you, chief,' said Trace in a broad cockney accent. 'Gotta bit of a problem. A blockage in the sewers. Things are starting to get nasty. I wonder if I could have a glance round your plumbing.'

'There's no problem here.'

'Not yet. But there will be. The rest of the gang's wandering about underneath in the sewers. I need to run some water through the pipes.'

'Well, I don't know . . .'

A right fucking jobsworth, thought Trace. 'It won't take long, chief. You can come with me if you like,' he said.

'I can't leave the monitors—'

'It *is* urgent. Otherwise we might have to declare the place a danger to health. And you know what that means.'

'I really need some authorization.' The commissionaire was starting to weaken.

Trace sighed and said, 'I'll call up the ganger,' took the radio from his pocket, switched it on and said, 'Steve. Problems at the Merc. Come back.'

When he pressed the receive button there was nothing but a burst of static.

'Shit,' said Trace, banging the radio with his hand. 'Bloody things never work round here. Too much metal.' And he repeated the exercise.

'Sorry, mate,' he said after a moment. 'That means I'll have to notify the depot. If I can't get in here now, we'll have to bang a restraint order on the place.'

The commissionaire hesitated, then said, 'Come on, then.' And he pulled the door open wide.

'Lovely,' said Trace. 'Won't be long.' He went over to the lifts and pressed the call button.

'Don't you want to go downstairs?' asked the commissionaire.

'Yeah, but I've got to look at the toilets upstairs first. You can keep an eye on me on the telly.' He nodded his head in the direction of the video monitors.

'We don't have cameras in the toilets,' said the commissionaire. 'Yet.'

'But you will,' said Trace with a friendly grin, as the lift arrived, and he stepped in smartly and pushed the button marked 3.

He was in and out of the gents on the third floor in a few seconds. The key had been where Yellow had said it would be, and with it in his possession, Trace went back to the ground floor.

'All OK upstairs,' he said. 'Just a quick look at your manholes down below and I'll be gone.'

'It's all locked up down there.'

'I don't want to go inside. The stuff I need's in the corridor.'

'All right, then.'

'Won't be long,' said Trace again, and he pushed through the door at the back of the reception hall and ran down the two flights to the basement.

The main door to the health club was covered by a security camera. Trace ignored it. He'd been in the club

66

before, and he went deeper into the labyrinth of corridors until he came to the back entrance to the club.

From the tool belt he extracted a set of lock picks, and was through the door within seconds. There were dim safety lights burning, but he knew there were no cameras or alarms inside, and he went to where the lockers were situated, opened the one he had the key for, secreted the envelope he found inside it under his waistcoat, and was back in the foyer within ten minutes.

'Cheers, mate,' he said to the commissionaire, touching the peak of his hard hat. 'Panic over. I think we've cleared the blockage.'

'Thank Christ for that,' said the uniformed man. 'The last thing I needed was to let the company know they had that sort of problem.'

'All part of the service,' said Trace as he went back out into the street. 'You pay enough rates here after all.'

And with that he was gone.

20

Trace found an empty pub by Greenwich Reach, stashed the hard hat, waistcoat and tool belt in the boot of the Cosworth, and went inside. He ordered a bottle of Becks, and moved towards a solitary table overlooking the width of the river.

He slit open the envelope with his thumbnail and emptied the contents on to the table top.

Inside were two more envelopes. One fat and one

thin. He opened the thin one first. It contained two pieces of A4 paper. The first was the profile of a man. Name, address, marital status, occupation, etc. The second simply contained an 0171 telephone number.

Trace opened the second envelope. It bulged with used fifty pound notes. He flicked through them. He counted ten thousand pounds. In with the money was a third A4 sheet. That one read BALANCE ON COMPLETION, and the number of one of Trace's Swiss bank accounts. He nodded with satisfaction. Yellow knew his terms. Trace looked out over the river that glistened in the morning sunshine. On the patio of the pub, a huge black crow stalked up and down the paved surface, occasionally pecking at some delicacy it saw between the stones, but mostly looking in at Trace with its sparkling black eyes. Trace left the hardly touched beer, went back out to his car and drove back to the house he had left that morning.

Once at home, he phoned the number on the second sheet of paper. It was answered on the second ring by a man who simply said, 'Hello.'

'Yellow,' said Trace.

'We need some information,' said the man's voice. 'I believe you can obtain it for us.'

'What information?'

'A date. A date when a very special person is coming into London Heathrow.'

'What person?'

'The leader of an Israeli hit squad. He has a job to do in England, and we don't want it to happen.'

'Name?'

'To your man he's known as David.'

'Just that?'

'Just that. We want flight details, immediate destination and the *nom de guerre* he's going to use whilst in this country.'

'Consider it done.'

'You're very confident.'

'I haven't failed yet.'

'When?'

'Within ten days.'

'That will do.'

'And I require proof of the balance of my fee being paid when I supply the information to you.'

'No problem. You have the deposit?'

'In front of me. Thank you.' Trace was calmer by then.

'A pleasure.'

'I'll call you on this number when the job's finished?'

'No one else has it, and it is manned twenty-four hours a day.'

'Until we speak again, then.' Trace put down the receiver, and began to make his plans for his next victim.

He was a Londoner, living in Hampstead with his second wife. His first lived in Berkshire with their two children, who the man visited on a fortnightly basis. He would go down on the Friday night in his Bentley Turbo, stay at a small but lavishly appointed hotel some twenty miles away from where his ex-wife lived, spend the next day with the children, which would culminate with a meal at the hotel, from which the kids would be collected by a limousine service and ferried home. The man then spent Saturday night at the hotel and drove himself home to his new wife in London early on Sunday morning.

Sunday morning it is, then, thought Trace.

And as the next day was Sunday, it was an ideal chance for a dummy run.

21

On that sunny Saturday morning, Detective Chief Inspector Jack Dancer was putting in some unpaid overtime at Peckham police station.

He looked at the fax on the desk in front of him that contained the details of the corpse found on Thursday afternoon.

The mutilated body had belonged to the manager of the main northern branch of one of the big five banks who had disappeared with the contents of the bank vaults, the not inconsiderable sum of three quarters of a million pounds, some five weeks earlier. A nationwide search had proved fruitless, a postcard had been received from Calais by his wife, Interpol had been brought in, but to no avail.

'So how the fuck did he end up at Dock Head trussed up like a Christmas turkey?' said Dancer to himself as his phone rang.

It was a female DS from Bermondsey. She told him that the mutilated body of a young girl had been found on the river's edge the previous afternoon and taken to St Thomas's hospital where she was in intensive care.

'And you're just telling me now,' shouted Dancer. 'What took you so long?'

'We didn't know you were to be informed,' said the DS huffily. 'There's nothing in the daily orders about it. One of your DCs on attachment to us said you'd been working on some similar cases.'

'Sorry, Sergeant,' said Dancer. 'You're quite right. Can she talk?'

'You haven't seen the state of her. I've never seen anything like it, and I hope I never do again.'

'That bad?'

'Worse. Whoever did this to her deserves being put out of his misery.'

'I'll come over now.'

'You'd better hurry, Inspector. She might not last too long.'

'I'm on my way,' said Dancer, and he hung up, then picked up the phone again and called Evans.

The phone was answered after eight rings. 'On the nest?' said the inspector when he recognized his sergeant's voice.

'I wish,' said Evans. 'Just doing a bit of upkeep on the old homestead.'

'Fancy doing some proper work for a change?'

'Come on, Guv, it's my day off.'

'Mine too. But I've turned in. I've got ID on the body we took a squint at the other day, and now a young girl's turned up, badly mutilated.'

'Fuck's sake. Same bloke?'

'Good bet.'

'He's keeping busy.'

'Isn't he just. Meet me at the ICU at St Thomas's.' Dancer slammed down his phone.

He was at the hospital within twenty minutes and,

after showing ID, was taken straight to the room where Trace's victim was lying, tubes protruding from what remained of her nose and mouth, the life-support machine she was hooked into showing just the merest signs of life with slow blips across its screen.

The female sergeant was sitting next to the girl's bed and stood up as Dancer entered and introduced himself.

'Christ on a bicycle,' said the inspector as he moved closer to the bed and looked at the girl's face. 'I see what you mean.'

'Not pretty is it, Guv?' said the sergeant.

'And she's said nothing?'

'Look at the state of her mouth.'

'Yeah. Sorry. And I apologize for flying off the handle earlier.'

'Forget it.'

'I'm expecting my sergeant,' said Dancer. 'I'll stay here if you like. You can take a break.'

'I could use a cuppa.'

'Go on then.'

The female officer left the room and Dancer moved her chair closer to the bed, sat down and looked closely at the girl. 'What did you ever do to deserve this?' he said aloud, and she moved her ruined eyes in his direction, spat out the tubes from her mouth, tried to sit up, then whispered through the wreckage of her mouth the single word 'mask' before falling back as the life-support machine went flat line.

Dancer leapt to his feet, ran to the door and threw it open. 'Nurse,' he yelled, and the sister on the desk outside ran in. She saw what had happened, hit the emergency pad that ran around the wall, picked up the phone and called for a resuscitation team.

It was too late. The girl was dead, and after five minutes the team gave up. Dancer, who had been standing watching their fruitless efforts, went outside and ran into Evans and the female DS.

At her look Dancer shook his head.

'Shit,' she said.

'You can get off now,' Dancer said to her. 'It's all over here. We'll take over from now.'

'OK, Guv,' said the woman. 'But get that bastard, won't you?'

'Count on it,' said the inspector, as the DS turned and walked wearily down the corridor.

Dancer and Evans went back into the ICU room where the staff were already preparing the girl to go for her post mortem, and Evans turned away in pity and disgust when he saw her condition.

'We *will* get him, won't we, Guv?' he said, echoing the DS's words.

'We'll try,' replied Dancer, not so confident now.

There was nothing they could do at that moment, so they went to the canteen for a cup of tea, and Dancer filled his sergeant in on developments.

'This is going from bad to worse,' said the inspector, when they were seated. 'You'll never guess who they pulled out of the river on Thursday.'

'No. But I'm sure you're going to tell me.'

'John Fawkes. Ring any bells?'

'Yeah. Who . . .?'

'The bank manager from Manchester who walked out with a big bag of money a month or so ago.'

'Christ. That's right. What the hell was he doing—'

'My thoughts exactly,' interrupted Dancer. 'When the news of his identity breaks, the station is going to be chocka. The papers love stories of bank managers going maverick. It makes their readers believe there is a Santa Claus. I'm going to get us put on an official status, so we don't have to answer a lot of damn fool, irrelevant questions. Now come on, let's get back to the station.'

They travelled in their separate cars, and when Evans walked into Dancer's office, he found him in conference with Jane King.

'Looks like we've got a new recruit,' said the inspector. 'There's something about cases like this that gets under people's skin. I'm going to get her seconded to the inquiry.'

'Hello, Jane,' said Evans. 'Welcome aboard. Not that it's exactly a pleasure cruise.'

'I'll survive,' said King.

'The PM's on the hurry up,' said Dancer. 'The body's already on the way to the morgue. Steve, you can drive.'

When they walked into the cold, sterile room, the chief pathologist himself was there, talking to the assistant that Dancer and Evans had met before, who gave them a cheery wave and unwrapped a Penguin biscuit.

The girl's body was lying naked on the slick metal of the examination table, her injuries now obvious for all to see. Jane King was forced to look away.

'I see you haven't lost your appetite,' said Dancer to the pathology assistant.

'We've all got to eat,' he replied as he bit off half the biscuit. He seemed rather hurt at Dancer's tone, and walked over to the bench that he favoured as a seat and picked up that morning's *Sun*.

'Good morning, Jack,' said the pathologist, ignoring his assistant's mood, and stripping the rubber glove off his right hand so that he could shake Dancer's. 'This is a nasty business.'

'And not the first.'

'Or the last if you ask me,' said the pathologist. 'Unless you lot get your collective fingers out. Whoever's doing this is a pure psychopath.'

'I know,' sighed Dancer as they walked together to look at the body. 'And there seems to be more of them out there every day. I'm getting too old for this lark. I can't just shrug them off as a part of the job like I used to. All this is beginning to get to me. Christ knows what these two kids are going to have to deal with in the future. I'll be glad when I'm retired and well out of it.'

'It's not getting any better, I'll give you that, Jack,' said the pathologist. 'Whoever had hold of this poor bitch really went to town on her.'

'There's just no logic to the choice of victim,' said Dancer. 'Maybe if I could find the common denominator there, I could get a handle on all this.'

'Well, the best of luck to you. Which is more than our friend here had. Any idea who she was?'

'Not so far,' said Dancer. 'She was naked when they found her. God. How could he?'

'Assuming of course that it was a he,' said the pathologist.

'I hope it is,' said Dancer. 'That a woman could do this to one of her own sex is unthinkable.'

'Have you ever seen photos of the guards at Treblinka?'

enquired the pathologist. 'Some women look very good in uniform. Speaking of which, who is the girl with you? Damn fine pectorals.'

'WPC Jane King,' replied Dancer. 'And I wouldn't let her hear you say that. Something of an independent soul is our Jane. And not frightened to call an old goat just that, whatever his position on the food chain.'

'Not so much of the old, Jack,' said the pathologist. 'So, let me introduce you to unknown woman number two hundred and ten. I've been saving the best bits just for you.'

'Thanks,' said Dancer dryly.

'Age: mid-twenties,' said the pathologist, his voice taking on a more serious tone now that it was time to get down to the nitty gritty. 'Height: five seven. Weight: eight stone twelve. A natural blonde as you can see, with a birth mark on her right hip roughly in the shape of a butterfly. She'd had her tonsils removed, and at some time she had broken her left ankle. She's had no children, but is not a virgin. But there is no evidence of recent sexual activity. So at least she wasn't raped. On very close examination I found that she'd been injected once in the heart and twice in the right arm. She must, however, have put up a fight, because there was a needle broken off in the bicep according to our friends at Tommy's.'

He saw the three police officers wince as one at the information. 'Sorry,' he said. 'From the blood sample I took she'd been pumped full of a strong anaesthetic and also a strong stimulant. I imagine in that order. One to send her to sleep, one to wake her up.'

'Professional,' said Dancer.

'Very,' replied the pathologist as he picked up a wicked-looking scalpel and cut a line from throat to groin, then the assistant passed him a power saw. The pathologist gestured for Dancer and his companions to step back, then thumbed the on button and started to cut through the bones of the girl's torso.

Pink water, blood and flesh fragments splashed over the pathologist's sleeve and the front of his hospital greens as the saw bit deeply.

He pulled open the chest cavity and signalled for the assistant to turn on the microphone that hung down over the examination table and was linked in with a voice-operated cassette recorder.

After he had cut out the vital organs, weighed and dissected them, all the time speaking his findings into the mike, the pathologist tore off his gloves and threw them into a garbage bin.

'I need a cigarette,' he said, to no one in particular. 'Let's go outside.'

When his Marlboro was lit to his satisfaction, he turned to the three officers who were standing with him in the corridor, and said, 'She had no chance, poor bitch.'

'What sort of creature could do a thing like that?' asked Jane King. 'Her poor head.'

'Looks like he put a blow lamp to it,' said the pathologist. 'She must've gone through hell before she finally died. I imagine she'd passed out, and then he stimulated her with the hypo to the heart.'

'God,' said Jane King. 'I hope I'm there when we catch him.'

'You will be,' said Dancer.

*

As he spoke the words, several miles away Trace was posting the video tape and photographs of the girl's last hours to a post office box in Paris. As the parcel left his fingers and dropped with a thud into the mail box, he shivered as if suddenly cold, even though the temperature was somewhere in the high seventies. The crow that was circling lazily above him let out a mournful cry, before banking away and heading towards central London.

22

The next morning, when Trace set off to the hotel in Berkshire to get a first glimpse of his next victim, the news that the Manchester bank manager had been found in the River Thames, tortured and dead, had broken in the Sunday papers.

Trace picked up the *Sunday Times* in a petrol station on the way, scanned the story, then threw the paper into the back seat of the Cosworth for a closer look later.

As he left London on the M4, which was virtually deserted at that hour, he put his foot down and the powerful, turbo-charged, de-tuned, racing engine of the Ford pushed the car to nearly 150 m.p.h., and Trace fought the steering wheel as the tyres almost left the tarmac.

He was at the hotel where the target was staying within the hour, and parked the Cosworth where he had a clear view of the car park and the huge, Racing Green Bentley Turbo that he was looking for.

An hour and a half later, when Trace had finished the paper, he saw a fattish, balding gent in a tan leather jacket over blue jeans that fitted too snugly around the crotch leave the front entrance of the hotel carrying an expensive-looking overnight bag and make his way to the Bentley.

He climbed aboard, fired up the engine and pulled smoothly out on to the A-road that led to the motorway through thick forest.

This is the place, thought Trace as he followed in the Ford. They soon reached the M4, then the Bentley sped back to London followed by the Cosworth. Trace hung well back as he tracked the big car through the main roads then the side streets to the target's home, where he garaged the Bentley. But the Torturer had spotted the place where he would snatch his victim, early, and retraced his route back to Berkshire to make his detailed plans.

He wasn't the only one busy that morning. At Peckham, Dancer had called an early morning conference with Evans and Jane King.

'Right,' he said, when they were both seated in front of him with cups of canteen coffee. 'This bloke's got to be caught pronto.' He tapped the pile of Sunday newspapers that sat on his desk. 'The Wapping wankers have had a field day with the ID of the latest victim. I said they would. And there's still no trace of the cash. Questions are being asked upstairs, and they've slung the whole lot into my ... *our* lap. From now on any intelligence about the identity of this geezer they're beginning to call the Torturer passes through this office first.'

'Has anybody any idea where he was holed up, between doing a runner and being put on the slab?' asked Evans.

'In a word – no,' said Dancer.

'Somebody did,' said Jane King.

'So we should try and turn that somebody up, shouldn't we?' said Dancer. 'Anyone fancy a day return to Manchester?'

Mariella Newman hadn't seen the newspapers. She rarely bothered with them these days, but she had heard the four o'clock news on GLR as she lay sleepless in her bed, running films of happier times through her head.

So he's struck again, she thought. More lives ruined. More destruction. More tears. More agony. Bastard. But even as her brain spun with hate, a terrible cold guilt began to cloak her like a blanket. She had done nothing to stop what had happened. And as she twisted and turned in turmoil, the crows that were roosted in her attic moved quietly from foot to foot as they felt her agony.

She rose from her bed, and walked with a rustle of her nightdress to the stairs that led upwards, and the crows moved as far away from the door as they could. They feared anyone with the power of sorcery. They feared the woman, they feared the Crow Man. But most of all they feared the one whose name only the bravest or most foolhardy human would dare to speak out loud. And deep down in their crow hearts they knew that battle would soon commence between those with the power, and only the strongest would survive.

The woman's fury was terrible to behold. She stood over the Crow Man who had been sleeping on the sofa, and screamed that she would see him brought to dust if he did not act quickly against the man who had destroyed her life.

'Have patience, mistress,' he begged, as she berated him for being a coward. 'Please. Everything will happen at its ordained time.'

'It had better,' she shrieked, before sweeping out of the attic and returning to her bedroom. 'Or you'll be bait for your own flea-bitten flock of carrion.'

23

The three police officers drove up to Manchester on Sunday afternoon. They found the bank manager's address with no trouble and Evans parked the car behind the traffic jam of TV news trucks and journalists' vehicles.

'Seems like we're not the first,' said Dancer dryly.

'What did you expect, Boss?' asked Evans.

'Just this. And for Christ's sake stop calling me Boss. How many more times have I got to tell you?'

'Sorry, Guv,' said the sergeant. 'What now?'

'Now we go and talk to the lady wife,' said Dancer, getting out of the car. 'Come on.'

They pushed past the gathering of newspapermen and

women, and the massed ranks of camera crews, towards the lone policeman guarding the gate to the house. As they approached he stepped forward and raised his hand. 'Right little Dixon of Dock Green, ain't he?' Evans muttered to King.

'Metropolitan Police,' Dancer announced to the uniformed constable and flashed his warrant card. 'Having fun?'

The young officer looked relieved to be talking to another policeman and said, 'Not too bad, sir.'

'Keep up the good work, then,' replied Dancer. 'Who's inside?'

'The wife and kids.'

'No more CID?'

'No. They've gone for now.'

'Good. Right. Keep this lot at bay.' He gestured back at the gathered newshounds. 'And you'll earn your money today.'

'They won't get past me,' said the young policeman who was tall and powerfully built.

'I believe they won't.' Dancer smiled, pushed open the gate and ushered his two juniors through. 'See you later, lad.'

Evans led the way up the path and knocked on the door. He knew the way Dancer liked to work.

After a minute a strained-faced woman answered the door. 'Yes?' she said.

It was Evans turn to show his credentials. 'Detective Sergeant Evans. CID,' he said. 'My colleagues: Detective Chief Inspector Dancer and Detective Constable King. We're up from London.'

'What do you want?'

Evans' demeanour softened. 'We're looking into the circumstances of your husband's death, Mrs Richards. We're sorry to bother you at this time, but your husband was found in our jurisdiction, and we're investigating the case down in London.'

'I didn't see you when I identified him.'

'No. You see, his murder is being linked with other incidents. Chief Inspector Dancer here is overseeing the entire operation.'

'You mean he might've been kidnapped? That it's not true what they've all been saying about him?'

Jane King interrupted. 'We don't want to talk about it out here do we, Mrs Richards? There are some pretty sophisticated listening devices around these days. Can we come inside?'

'I'm sorry,' said the bank manager's wife. 'Of course you can. Come in.'

She led them into a comfortable-looking sitting room with the curtains drawn over the windows facing on to the front garden.

'I can't bear those people staring in,' she said. 'They went away for a bit, but now there seem to be dozens of them out there.'

'I'm afraid that was bound to happen.' Dancer spoke for the first time.

'I suppose,' said Mrs Richards. 'Would you like some coffee?'

'If it's not too much trouble,' said Dancer. 'It's a long drive up from London.'

'It won't take a minute,' and the woman left the room.

'Poor cow,' said Evans when she was gone.

'Quite,' said Dancer. 'Let's keep this as friendly as

83

possible. The reports from the local CID reckon she knew nothing about hubby going AWOL, and I tend to agree. Otherwise the whole bloody family would've pissed off to Spain, or somewhere, together. I reckon he did the deed off his own bat. I want to know if there was another woman involved. Reports say not. But I'm always suspicious when an otherwise respectable middle-aged man goes wally. Jane, you talk to her. I'll listen.'

When Mrs Richards returned with a tray carrying a coffee pot, milk, sugar, biscuits, and four cups and saucers, Jane King took it from her and put it on the table. 'Sit down, Mrs Richards,' she said. 'I'll pour. How are you feeling?'

'Terrible.'

Jane King regarded her seriously. 'We're all very sorry. And I mean that.'

'Do you think he was kidnapped, and the money stolen?' asked Tanya Richards again.

'We don't know,' said Jane King, handing her a cup of coffee. 'We have to find out where your husband was from the time he disappeared until he was found. That'll be a start.'

'I have no idea. I really don't. He just went off in his car as usual one Thursday morning. I wasn't worried until he didn't get home in time for dinner. I called the bank, but only the security man was there. I waited until midnight before phoning the police. They found his car in its usual parking spot. Then they called in the bank inspector and they opened up the vault and found—'

That the cupboard was bare, thought Dancer, but didn't vocalize his thoughts. 'We know,' he said.

'It was awful,' said Tanya Richards. 'The suspicions. I've been cut dead by some of my best friends.'

That's what friends are for, thought Dancer. 'Don't distress yourself, Mrs Richards,' he said. 'Please.'

'How can I *not* distress myself? My husband's dead. Not distressing myself won't bring him back.'

The words hung in the air like the crow that was floating over the house, beating its wings lazily against the updraft of warm air that rose from the city.

'Of course,' said Jane King, shooting a look at Dancer. 'Was your husband doing anything out of character before he disappeared?'

'No,' said Tanya Richards. 'We led a quiet life. Just us and the children. Are you asking if he was having an affair?'

'It had occurred to us,' replied the female police officer gently.

'Do you think the other police didn't ask me? I've racked my brian since he went, and I can't believe that he was,' said Tanya Richards. 'He lived for us. The family. He was regular in his habits and he did nothing unusual at all. He went to work and came home. That was his life.' She started to cry then, and Jane King gave her some clean tissues.

'So you can think of nothing that would have brought on his disappearance?' Dancer pressed. 'No debts? Gambling? Anything?'

'Not John,' said Tanya Richards. 'He wouldn't even buy a ticket for the lottery, and he refused to have credit cards.'

'Well, I'm sorry to have bothered you, Mrs Richards,' said Jack Dancer, getting to his feet, and taking a card

85

from inside his wallet. 'This is my private number. If you do think of anything, please don't hesitate to call it. And please accept my condolences on your loss.'

'Catch him,' said Tanya Richards through gritted teeth. 'Whoever did that to John deserves to be caught and punished. And there are others, aren't there?'

'We think so.'

'Who could do that? Such terrible, unthinkable things. He was a kind man. A gentle man. He never hit the kids, however naughty they'd been. He always just talked to them. Man to man. They're broken hearted. The doctors didn't want me to see his body when I went down to London, but I insisted. It was horrible. My poor love.'

'I really am sorry, Mrs Richards,' said Dancer. 'We'll get the person who did it, believe me.'

But as he left the house where the woman stayed sobbing on the sofa in the living room, he was not so sure.

24

The identity of the girl who had died on Saturday morning at St Thomas's was waiting on Dancer's desk when he got into work on Monday morning. Penelope Bannister lived in Battersea. She had been reported missing after not turning up for work on Friday. A male colleague, who had been having an on–off affair with her, which he would have preferred to have been more serious, had called her flat and, on getting only her answering machine, had driven to the block during his lunchtime. After explaining the situation to the security men there, he had persuaded them to check the car park. They had found her Golf neatly parked in its designated slot and gone upstairs to her apartment. After knocking and ringing for ten minutes, one of the security men had fetched the duplicate key to the front door, and all three had gone inside.

The flat had been empty and undisturbed with no sign that she had returned the previous evening. The answering machine revealed timed messages from Thursday night still waiting to be played, and so her male colleague returned to the office where he obtained her parents' phone number in Basingstoke from Penelope's personal file and tried them. They were as mystified as he was, and reluctantly they informed the local police. The report was transferred to Scotland Yard, and a trawl round the London hospitals and morgues finally turned up unknown woman number two hundred and ten in the south London mortuary on Saturday evening.

The parents had been driven up from Basingstoke on Sunday morning, but in deference to their advancing years, the male colleague from Penelope Bannister's office had agreed to view the body first, in case it was not her, in order not to upset the elderly couple unnecessarily.

The man vomited his breakfast down his impeccably pressed, pre-faded Levi's and his expensive suede ankle boots when he saw the body of his sometime lover. He was led outside to sit on the wall and shakily smoke a cigarette while the parents were informed.

The mother insisted on seeing her daughter's body

despite advice from the policeman and woman in attendance. When she did look at Penelope Bannister's mutilated and burned corpse, she had a heart seizure and was rushed to St Thomas's herself, where she died later that evening, adding yet another scalp to the Torturer's growing list.

Dancer mulled over the information as his coffee grew cold, and the bacon roll he had eaten burned inside his stomach at the injustice of it all. As soon as Evans and King made an appearance all three went off to Penelope Bannister's place of work. Once there they interviewed the male colleague whose name was Mark Russell, who nervously smoked and chewed his nails throughout.

'Mr Russell,' said Dancer, 'when did you last see Miss Bannister?'

'I already told the other policemen.'

'I understand that, Mr Russell. But this is a serious matter, as you must appreciate. Please bear with us. We'll try to make this as painless as possible for you. We realize what a shock it was for you to see the body. Now, when was it?'

'On Thursday evening,' said Mark Russell. 'We went for a few drinks at the P45.' At the police officers' mystified looks he explained: 'That's what we call our local bar. When anyone's going to get the sack, they always get taken there for lunch first.'

'I see,' said Dancer. 'And she left alone?'

'That's right,' said Russell, lighting another in a chain of Marlboros, and ignoring the sign on the wall that said: THIS IS A SMOKE FREE ZONE. 'At about eight, I suppose. Something like that. I wanted to take her out to dinner. But she said she was tired and had some M&S stuff to eat.'

'She didn't offer to share it with you?' asked Jane King.

'No. I wish she had ... Or come out with me ... Perhaps then none of this would have happened ... Who could do such a thing? She was a lovely girl.'

'You were having a relationship with her?' Evans this time.

'No. Yes. Sort of. We'd gone out a few times.'

'But she wasn't keen?' Evans again.

'She didn't want to be tied down.' Russell looked at the sergeant. 'You don't think I—'

'No, Mr Russell, we don't,' said Dancer firmly. 'The other officers have checked on your whereabouts when Miss Bannister was murdered. And everything that happened to her fits in with the *modus operandi* of someone else we're anxious to find.'

'Not that bloke who was in the paper yesterday? The Torturer, or whatever they call him?'

'Precisely.'

'But why would he want to hurt Penny?'

'That's exactly what we'd like to know. So as far as you were concerned she went straight home?'

'That's what she said. A meal, a bath and to bed with the TV.'

And you'd rather it was you, Mark, thought Jane King, feeling rather sorry for him.

'But she didn't make it,' said Evans.

'Her car was in the car park.'

'But there was no sign of her shopping anywhere. Not in the car or in the flat. It has been searched thoroughly.

89

She got as far as the car park, and then vanished into thin air.'

Russell nodded miserably.

'And nothing suspicious had taken place recently?' asked Dancer.

'How do you mean?'

'Had Penny reported seeing any strange characters hanging about either here or at home? Or said she'd been followed, or received any strange phone calls or letters?'

'No. She was in fine form.'

'Very well, Mr Russell,' said Dancer, taking one of his cards from his pocket. 'If by any chance you do think of anything, please call me. My office number is on the top, my home number at the bottom. Any time, night or day. Please don't hesitate.'

'I won't,' said Russell, stubbing out his umpteenth cigarette. 'Can I get back to work now?'

'Are you sure you're up to it?' asked Jane King kindly. 'You have been through an unsettling experience. Maybe you should take some time off.'

'No,' said Russell. 'I think I'd prefer to work. So, can I go?'

Dancer nodded, and Russell left the room. 'Let's get out of here and take a look at her flat,' said Dancer.

But a close search of the apartment, and an examination of the VW brought nothing to light. Trace had made sure that any sign of his surveillance was long gone before he'd snatched Penny Bannister, and the security men on duty that Thursday evening had heard and seen nothing unusual.

25

The rest of the week passed slowly and routinely for the main players in the drama. Matt Trace prepared his torture room for the next victim. Dancer, Evans and King pulled in every snout they had, and called in every favour they were owed from villains and upright citizens alike, to try and get information on the Torturer, but to no avail. Mariella Newman stayed inside her house and mourned her dead family, and the Crow Man sat in the attic, listening to his feathered spies as they cawed the information they had gathered into his ears.

Early the following Sunday morning Trace dressed himself in his police uniform, chose an air pistol from the collection of weapons he kept in Peckham, cleaned, oiled and loaded it with a single anaesthetic dart, put it in a shoulder holster under his jacket, and took the Ford Mondeo police car up the motorway to Berkshire. Even though the car was in the livery of a Metropolitan Police vehicle, he didn't expect his target to notice. A police car was a police car to the civilian population, and he was sure that it would convince his victim that he was genuine.

He pulled up on the forest road close to the motorway, just beside the entrance to a lane leading nowhere but to a deserted clearing that he had discovered the previous Sunday, and which, by the litter of used condoms and fast-food containers he'd seen, was obviously used by the local young people as a trysting place. After checking that the clearing was empty, he turned the car to face the direction of the hotel, with its headlights on full beam, its emergency lights flashing and the blue police lamps spinning on top. As he waited for the Bentley, only one other car passed him, the driver craning his neck to see what was going on. Trace waved him on.

Five minutes later the green Turbo crested the brow of the hill and glided towards Trace. He stepped forward, hand upraised and the car slid to a halt, the electric driver's window rolled down, and his victim looked out. 'Something wrong, officer?' he asked from the comfort of the leather and polished walnut interior.

'Crash up ahead, sir,' said Trace. 'A bad one. The road's blocked.'

'Damn. How do I get back to the motorway?'

'Easily, sir. Just take that turning.' Trace gestured towards the lane. 'That'll lead you to the Newbury road, and it's signposted from there.'

'Thank you, officer,' said the man, and did as he was told. Trace watched the car lurch up the lane, jumped back into the Mondeo, turned off the lights and followed it.

He found the Bentley sitting in the clearing with his target standing beside it, scratching his head in puzzlement. 'Thank goodness you've come, officer,' said the target. 'I seem to be lost. I must've taken a wrong turning.'

'No you haven't, Mr Goldstein.'

'How the devil do you know my name?' said Goldstein, alarm flaring in his eyes.

'I know everything about you,' said Trace as he

unbuttoned his tunic, took the anaesthetic gun from under it and shot his target in the neck. 'Everything.'

As the dart hit Goldstein in the flab under his chin, the crow sitting in a tree above did a furious little dance before taking off and heading east.

Trace re-holstered the gun, went over to the fallen man, took the dart from his neck and carefully put it into his pocket, then dragged Goldstein over to the Mondeo and shoved him into the gap between the back and front seats and covered him with a blanket. According to his calculations on the man's body weight, the anaesthetic should keep him unconscious for just over two hours.

In fact it was exactly two hours and eight minutes later when Goldstein opened his eyes.

'Hello, Gerry,' said Trace. 'Welcome to my world.'

The fat man licked his lips and said, as they almost all said when confronted with the Torturer, 'Who are you? What do you want?'

'I'm your future, Gerry,' Trace said gently. 'And unless you tell me what I want to know, it's going to be a very short future indeed.'

'I don't know what you're talking about. Let me go.'

They were in the factory in Peckham. Gerry Goldstein was naked, tied hand and foot and lying on the cold stone floor. Trace was sitting on a straight-backed kitchen chair looking down at him. The sun poured through the filthy windows and bathed the whole place in a warm, dusty glow, but Goldstein shivered as he looked up at his captor.

'This is madness,' he said. 'You must have the wrong man.'

Trace shook his head. 'No, Gerry,' he said. 'Now, if you tell me when David is coming into the country, you can avoid any more discomfort.'

'I don't know anyone called David.'

Trace kicked him in the soft flesh that covered his ribs. It was not a hard kick but Goldstein squealed, and for the first time seemed to appreciate his own nakedness. 'Don't,' he said, and his voice was a pitch higher than before.

'Of course you do,' said Trace. 'Everyone knows *someone* called David. But this is a very special David. He's coming to England soon on a mission. I want to know when, what name he's using, and where he's going to stay once he gets here.'

Fear flared again in Goldstein's eyes, and he shook his head rapidly. 'No,' he said thickly. 'No.'

'Yes,' pressed Trace.

'I swear I don't know what you're talking about.'

'I swear that you do, and I also swear that you'll soon tell me.' Trace got up from his seat and went over to the bench attached to the wall.

On it was an electric baton made in the Jing Jiang Radio No. 4 factory in Jiangsu, China. It was roughly the length of a vibrator and shaped for easy insertion into the body. But instead of pleasure, its object was pain. Severe pain. Next to it was a tube of KY Jelly.

Trace picked them both up and explained the application of the baton as he returned to where Goldstein was lying. He rolled the fat man over, knelt and applied the jelly to the barrel of the implement.

The fat man whimpered. 'God no. You can't. I have a weak heart.'

'Then tell me,' said Trace. 'And save yourself the discomfort.'

'I don't know anything . . .' insisted Goldstein.

Trace inserted the prod into his anus, pushed hard until the implement was half inserted into his body, and said. 'Are you sure?'

'Of course I am.'

'Liar.'

'No. I swear—'

'Don't. You'll be wasting your breath.'

'I'll give you anything.'

'The truth will do.'

'But I don't—' And Trace thumbed the button on the electric implement.

Goldstein screamed as the electrical charge contained in the prod ripped at his insides. Sweat broke out from every pore on his body, and he crabbed across the rough concrete to escape from the agony, tearing the skin off his upper arm, hips and legs as he went.

Trace grabbed him by his thinning hair, and asked, 'Memory coming back?'

Goldstein started to cry, but still professed his innocence of anyone called David.

Once again Trace pushed the button on the prod, and once again the charge seared the delicate tissue of Goldstein's back passage. Involuntarily he urinated, and his eyes bulged as if they were going to burst out of their sockets, but still he remained silent.

Trace pulled the baton from Goldstein's hole and

dragged the man away from the pool of piss in which he was lying.

'You're tougher than you look,' he said. 'But not tough enough. I think I'll just leave you to think about it for a bit.'

He fetched a set of heavy manacles from the bench, then pulled a flick knife from his pocket and cut the rope that held Goldstein's wrists. Before the man could regain any feeling in his hands and retaliate, Trace twisted one arm behind his back, pulled his other arm over his shoulder and manacled that too. Then he lowered a chain with a wicked-looking hook at the end from the ceiling, hooked the end into the chain of the manacles and hauled Goldstein up until his feet left the floor.

The pain the fat man felt was indescribable as his arms were yanked up tight, and he started to wail. Trace ignored his cries, and went and got a bottle of water from the fridge upstairs.

He sat and drank it as he watched Goldstein pivot slowly at the end of the chain, his eyes popping and his breath catching in his chest with the agony, and his cries becoming fainter.

That Sunday lunchtime passed slowly for both of them, until at about two in the afternoon Trace allowed the fat man some respite by lowering him to the floor again.

Goldstein's left shoulder was dislocated, and he shrieked as it touched the floor.

Trace worked the dislocated bone against the edge of the socket and Goldstein fainted.

Shit, he thought, and prepared a hypodermic of adrenalin to resuscitate his victim, hoping that his heart would stand it.

Goldstein came awake with a jolt, and Trace said, 'Remembered anything yet, Gerry?'

The fat man shook his head.

'OK, then. Now we get serious.'

Trace pulled a length of black plastic from the roll under the bench and laid it on the floor, rolled Goldstein on top of it, then undid the manacles.

Trace looked at the circumcised penis between Goldstein's legs and grinned a cold grin.

'You're going to cut your own prick off unless you tell me what I want to know.'

Goldstein paled visibly and began to shake all over as if with ague. 'No,' he pleaded. 'No. For pity's sake.'

'There is no pity in here,' said Trace.

'Why are you doing this?' asked Goldstein.

'Because it's my job,' replied the Torturer. 'It's all that I know.'

Trace went to the magnetic strip he had screwed to the wall and pulled off a huge pair of shears. He went back to where Goldstein was sitting and tossed them on to the floor next to him. 'Pick them up,' he ordered.

Goldstein shook his head.

'Right,' said Trace. 'These are the alternatives. Do what I tell you and you have a chance to live. Afterwards I'll get you to a hospital. Otherwise . . .' He went to one of the drawers in the bench, unlocked it and brought out a nine-millimetre Beretta automatic. He inserted a fresh clip of fifteen brass-jacketed bullets into the butt of the gun and screwed a silencer to the barrel. 'Otherwise,' he went on, 'I kill you, and forfeit the balance of my fee.'

'You wouldn't,' said Goldstein.

'Wouldn't I?' asked Trace, aimed the gun at the fat man's head and squeezed the trigger.

The man jerked back, screamed 'No,' and expelled a thick stream of liquid faeces across the black plastic as the suppressed sound from the shot echoed around the factory's walls.

Trace pulled a face at the stench. The cartridge case from the blank round bounced across the concrete floor, twinkling as the sun caught it.

'April fool,' he said. 'The next one's real.'

Goldstein grabbed the shears and threw them at Trace, who dodged them easily, and planted his boot in Goldstein's ribs. 'Fetch,' he ordered.

'No,' said the fat man, the shit already beginning to dry on his legs.

Trace kicked him again and again, forcing him to crawl in the direction of the shears. 'Do it, you bastard,' shouted Trace.

As Goldstein got closer to the implement and the tattoo of vicious boot blows continued, he realized that Trace was serious, and all the fight went out of the fat man. 'All right, all right,' he protested. 'I'll tell you.'

'Tell me what?' Trace was hardly out of breath.

'What you want to know. About David.'

'Good.'

Goldstein hesitated.

'Go on then,' said Trace. 'Or I'll cut it off for you myself.'

Goldstein started to cry again. 'He's coming in from Israel via Paris on the tenth,' he sobbed. 'BA flight ten twenty-four, due to arrive at Heathrow at midday. He's using an American passport in the name of Webb. Hannibal Webb. And he's got a suite booked at the Ritz for a week. Now are you satisfied?'

'Thank you,' said Trace. 'And I hope you're telling the truth.'

'I am.'

'Good. Stand up and sit on the chair.' Trace indicated the kitchen chair that he'd been sitting on when Goldstein awoke.

'Can't I go home now?' asked Goldstein pathetically.

'Not until after the tenth.'

'What? That's six days away.'

'You could be lying.'

'No.'

Trace thought about it. 'Very well,' he said. 'I'll check. Sit.'

Goldstein did as he was told. Trace manacled him to the chair and gagged him with gaffer tape. He took the magazine out of the Beretta, unscrewed the silencer, and locked all three pieces back in the drawer. Pocketing the key, Trace went upstairs and picked up one of several portable telephones that he kept there.

He called up the same number as he'd used when accepting the job, and as far as he could tell, the same voice answered.

'Hello,' said the voice.

'Yellow,' said Trace.

'Yes.'

'I have what you need.'

'Tell me.'

'The money.'

'The information.'

'One of us has to trust the other I suppose.'

'Precisely.'

'Very well, I'll trust you. You know what will happen if you betray that trust.' And Trace supplied the details as Goldstein had given them to him.

'Good,' said the voice.

'Can you check? I don't want him giving me any false information.'

'It will be done.'

Trace gave him the number of the portable and the voice said, 'I'll contact you again within the hour,' then hung up.

Trace took the phone and another cold bottle of water downstairs to where Goldstein was waiting, sipping the icy liquid as the sun crept across the sky, and the shadows inside the factory lengthened.

Exactly one hour later the phone rang. Trace answered, and the voice said, 'Yellow.'

'Go ahead,' said Trace.

'It computes,' said the voice. 'I think we have our man.'

'Good,' said Trace. 'The balance of the money?'

'On its way.'

'Good,' said Trace again.

'Your informant cannot be allowed to jeopardize our next move.'

'Don't worry, he won't.' And this time it was Trace's turn to break the connection.

26

Trace put down the phone, went over to Goldstein, ripped off the tape and said, 'Looks like you were telling the truth.'

The fat man hung his head in shame.

'So what shall I do with you now?'

Goldstein lifted his head. 'Don't you care?' he asked.

'About what?'

'David. He is coming here to rid the world of an evil man.'

'Sez you. Evil is a relative term.'

'Believe me, he is.'

'I couldn't care less.'

'What do you care about?'

'Not your race or religion. Or your politics. I care for myself. Myself and money. And lately, not even that very much. Or myself if you must know.' He shrugged.

'Bastard.'

'Which doesn't answer my question. What am I going to do with you now?'

'Let me go. You've got what you want.'

'And allow you to warn our man? I don't think so. I don't believe my principals would appreciate that.'

'You can't keep me here.'

'I have no intention of doing that.'

Realization dawned on Goldstein's face. 'You can't.'

'Why not?'

'That's murder.'

'It won't be the first time nor, I hope, the last.' Trace laughed another of his mirthless laughs.

'Who *are* you?' asked Goldstein.

'Your nemesis.'

Trace returned yet again to the bench and picked up a washing-up liquid bottle and weighed it in his hand. It was heavy. He had filled it with petrol during his preparations for Goldstein.

'Thirsty?' he asked.

Goldstein nodded.

'Have a drink on me, then.' Trace carried it over to the seated man.

'What is it?'

'Four star unleaded.'

'*What?*'

'You heard. Now have a sip.'

'No.' And Goldstein closed his mouth firmly.

Trace squeezed the toxic liquid into his face, and Goldstein vainly tried to dodge out of the way as the petrol seared his skin and eyes.

'No,' he choked spitting petrol and mucus, dripping from his nose, off his lips.

'Yes.'

'You can't.' Goldstein moved so violently that the chair tipped over and deposited him on the floor with a bone-shaking thud.

Trace half-emptied the Squeezy bottle over the big man's body, then took a red tipped match out of his pocket and ignited it with his thumb nail.

Goldstein looked up at the spark through red rimmed eyes, as if mesmerized. 'No,' he bellowed. 'For God's sake have mercy.'

Trace smiled and flipped the match in his direction. Over and over it turned in the air, its tiny flame fluttering as it floated lightly towards the petrol vapour that shimmered in the air above Goldstein's body. The vapour caught with a whumph, and his torso flashed as the fire took hold. He screeched for the last time then, so loudly that the crows sitting on the roof fluttered away from their perch, and so violently that his body and the chair to which he was still bound lifted clean off the floor.

27

Trace watched as Goldstein burned; black smoke from his seared flesh rose to the high ceiling of the factory, and the smell of cooking flesh assaulted his nose. He moved away from the heat and stink, mesmerized by the sight of the fat man flailing around, until the spilt petrol began to threaten the walls of the building, and he picked up a foam-filled fire extinguisher and doused Goldstein's body and the concrete floor around it.

The fire was immediately extinguished, and Goldstein lay moaning, his limbs like charcoal. Trace went to the drawer again, unlocked it and reconstructed the Beretta. He walked over to the body, put the end of the silencer against Goldstein's head and squeezed the trigger gently. The fat man's body jerked as the heavy bullet tore half his head off, and he died instantly with a spasm of his arms and legs.

'I told you the next one would be real,' said Trace, who split the gun again, returned it to the drawer and locked it, then started to dispose of Goldstein's body.

First he pulled on thick rubber gloves, then he got another length of plastic and dropped it over the corpse, chair and all. He rolled the still-hot cadaver into the plastic and secured it with gaffer tape. He went to the garage door and got a trolley, came back, loaded Goldstein on board and wheeled him back to the Transit. He lifted the body and dropped it on to the flat bed and slammed the doors.

Then, grimacing at the foul smell, threw the gloves, gun and the portable phone into the cab, and started up the motor. He drove out of the factory and turned east, following the river until he came to a public refuse tip run by Southwark Council. He drove to the centre, got out of the truck, looked around quickly, put the gloves back on, then opened the back doors, tugged the body out and dropped it into a pile of black-plastic-covered garbage.

He drove off the site, returned the way he had come until he turned off the main street and into a service road between two factories, found the tow path and dropped the gloves, the gun and telephone into the murky waters of the river.

Having completed his task, he went back to Greenwich for a change of clothing, with the two crows flapping behind his car at roof-top height.

The body was discovered late on Monday afternoon by two teenage boys looking for excitement and treasure on the tip. They found the former, but not the latter, at least not until they both sold their stories to the *Sun*.

Dancer and King were in the office, and Evans was pumping an informant in a pub in Rye Lane when the news came through.

Dancer immediately called Evans out of his meeting and arranged to pick him up.

'Anything?' asked Evans as Jane King steered the car expertly through the narrow streets close to the river.

'No. Just that this one has been burnt. But not until after he had been chained to a wooden chair.'

'God almighty.'

'But before he was shot in the head at point blank,' said King from the front seat.

'Son of a bitch.'

'Well put, Steve,' said Dancer.

Goldstein's body was still *in situ* at the garbage dump when the trio arrived. Yellow tape slung between four stakes stuck in the dirt cordoned off the area, whilst a dozen police constables in one-piece overalls did a fingertip search of the ground.

'Fat chance of finding anything useful in this lot,' said Dancer disgustedly as he surveyed the piles of rubbish strewn around.

The plastic had been carefully cut from the body, and was undergoing a swift fingerprinting before being taken to the police lab, but as, once again, Trace had been wearing gloves throughout, there would be no useful evidence found.

The body itself, still chained to the skeleton of the chair, had been transferred to the back of a mortuary wagon for a brief pathological examination before transfer to the mortuary for a full post mortem.

The same pathologist who had done the PM on

Penelope Bannister was in attendance. 'Another fine mess, Jack,' he muttered.

Dancer nodded as he looked at the horror of Goldstein's blackened body. The smell of the cooked flesh caught at the back of his throat and made him want to vomit.

'It's pretty obvious how he died,' said the pathologist, gesturing at the ruin that had been the man's head. 'Unless of course he was dead from shock or the burns beforehand, and the killer just wanted to make sure.'

'He was still alive,' said Dancer. 'Our man's not the type to waste a bullet. Is it still in there, by the way?'

'I don't think so. I imagine it went right through when it blew the side of his head off. And from what I can gather, even if it hadn't, our man, as you call him, would happily have gone in and retrieved it.'

'Too bloody true,' said Evans from behind Dancer. 'This sod doesn't give a fuck.'

'Quite,' said the pathologist. 'I'm going to take him back to the mortuary where I can get a proper look. Will you be down later, Jack?'

'We'll be there,' said Dancer. 'I just want to have a squint round here first.'

But the police at the site came up with nothing as they disturbed the crows that strutted about amongst the garbage.

'Mortuary or office?' asked Jane King as she kicked off her Wellington boots, stuck them in the boot of the car, and put her shoes back on.

'Office, I think,' said Dancer. 'We can check the PM later. The bloke's dead, and that's all we need to know for now. I'd rather try and find out who he is. Or was.'

'Not much chance of an eyeball or fingerprint ID,' said Evans.

'We'll have to check the dentists, then. Another bloody long job.'

But it wasn't to be as long a job as they thought. Almost as soon as they were back in Dancer's office, with tea and cigarettes going, he got a call from Special Branch.

'Hello, Jack, Danny Lonegan here. I understand you've got a body.'

'I've got loads. Which one do you want?'

'The one that was found charcoal grilled in Southwark this afternoon.'

'Oh yeah. What's your interest, Danny?'

'Well, we've got a report that a certain Gerald Simon Goldstein went missing yesterday. His missus phoned her local nick at Hampstead when he didn't get back for Sunday lunch. Seems he's a man of very regular habits. Every Saturday he visits the kids from his first marriage down in Berkshire. Stays at the same hotel, arrives back in London on Sunday morning. Like clockwork, according to the wife. Anyway, he checked out of the hotel as usual yesterday, first thing, then vanished. Last night the Newbury coppers got a report that a car had been abandoned in the local lovers' lane close to the hotel. It was his. It's pretty distinctive. A green Bentley Turbo. The woodentops checked it out. It was unlocked and empty. Keys gone. They had it towed in. No sign of Goldstein or a struggle or anything. And we were wondering if there might be a connection to your stiff.'

'And what's the particular Special Branch interest in this one?'

'This bloke is one of the richest Jewish businessmen in London, and he's well in with Mossad. As you can imagine, there's a bit of a panic on.'

'Christ,' said Dancer.

'So, do you mind if we take a shufti? We might be able to come up with a swift ID for you.'

'Course, mate,' said Dancer. 'Any help would be appreciated. It's been taken down to Waterloo. Why don't we meet there in . . .' He looked at his watch, '. . . one hour.'

'I'll be there, Jack. See you then.' And Danny Lonegan hung up.

'Shit,' said Dancer, as he put down the receiver. 'That's all we need. A bloody political connection. This is turning into a nightmare.'

28

The Great Beast stirred and woke from its long slumber. It looked at the world and was glad at what it saw. Chaos reigned supreme, and the Beast was pleased. It lay back, made the devil's sign with the forefinger and little finger of its left hand and listened as the long-awaited message was delivered by one of the imps of hell. And the Beast roared with pleasure and spat out a gout of flame from its monstrous mouth that turned the imp instantly to ash.

That evening, as Evans drove King and Dancer to the morgue, Matt Trace returned to the factory to clear up the previous day's mess. He found the bullet that had killed Goldstein embedded in the concrete where it had finished up, dug it out with a chisel and dropped it into the burner, then doused down the floor with water and scrubbed it clean of blood and foam. Then he returned home to catch up on his sleep.

When the three CID officers got to Waterloo, Commander Danny Lonegan was already there with his DI, Patricia Smylie. 'Hello, Danny, Pat,' said Dancer. 'You both know DS Evans I believe, and this is DC Jane King. She's come on board the investigation.'

The two Special Branch officers nodded their greetings and Lonegan said, 'Shall we take a look, Jack?'

'He's pretty bad,' said Dancer. 'How you going to ID him?'

'His teeth,' said Lonegan. 'He's got a couple of gold molars at the back.'

'Told you,' said Evans. 'I knew the only way would be through his hampsteads.'

'I just hope you can find them,' said Dancer. 'Half his head's gone.'

The five of them went through to the pathology room where the PM had just been completed.

'Just as I thought, Jack,' said the pathologist. 'He was still alive when he was shot. He must've been through hell. It was a mercy to put him out of his misery.'

'I don't think our man's got an ounce of mercy in him,' replied Dancer. 'He probably just wanted to get it over and done with so he could have his dinner. What time did it happen?'

'Sunday evening as far as I can tell,' said the pathologist, and Lonegan nodded in satisfaction.

Dancer introduced him and Smylie, and the Commander asked, 'How's his jaw?'

'Fine,' replied the pathologist. 'The bullet went right through the upper part of his cranium leaving the teeth intact.'

'Good,' said Lonegan. 'Any gold fillings?'

'Two. Bottom right.'

'It's our man all right,' said Lonegan. 'Gerald Simon Goldstein.'

'Right,' said Dancer. 'We'd better go and have a word with his wife. No objections, Danny?'

'None. But keep us informed. We'd better get back to the Yard and let them know we've found our man.'

'But not his killer,' said the pathologist.

'In time,' said Dancer testily. 'In time.'

The trio drove up to the address that Lonegan supplied and arrived at about eight-thirty. It was still light, and from the heights of Hampstead they saw the evening smog lying over London like smoke in an ashtray.

'It doesn't get any better,' said Jack Dancer gloomily.

'No. But it helps if you live in a place like this,' said Evans as he surveyed the Goldstein residence.

'Not if you get burnt to a crisp and shot for it,' remarked Jane King, as Evans parked the car and they all got out.

Dancer pushed the button on the entryphone next to the front gates and after a moment a female voice answered. He identified himself and the voice said, 'Come in.'

The gates swung open noiselessly and they walked up the tiled path to the front door.

It was answered by a uniformed policewoman. 'Constable Gratton, sir,' she introduced herself. 'I'm taking care of Mrs Goldstein.'

'Can we talk?' he asked.

Gratton nodded. 'She can't hear.'

'How is she?' asked Dancer.

The constable shrugged. 'Not good.'

'She's going to be worse after we talk to her. Where's her doctor?'

'Down the hill. Private.'

'Might be a good idea to call him.'

'Is Mr Goldstein . . .?' She didn't finish the sentence, but he knew what she meant.

Dancer nodded.

'That's a shame. She seems nice. What happened?'

'A bad one. He was taken by the bloke they're calling the Torturer.'

'God.'

'There wasn't much godly about what happened,' said Evans. 'He was a right mess when we found him. Where's Mrs Goldstein now?'

'Upstairs, lying down.'

'You'd better fetch her,' said Dancer. 'Then maybe you could call her doctor and make some tea.'

'Something stronger might be better,' said Jane King.

'Both,' said Dancer. 'Now, constable. Show us to the sitting room.'

Gratton did as she was told, then went upstairs and fetched Judith Goldstein.

She was dark and beautiful, a full twenty years younger than her husband, according to Lonegan. Trophy wife, thought Dancer as he stood and greeted her. He ushered her to a seat on the sofa that faced a picture window looking out over an enormous stretch of garden which must have doubled the value of the house.

He introduced Evans and King, who had also risen at Judith Goldstein's entrance. Gratton whispered that she would make them all tea, and vanished into the kitchen.

When Goldstein's wife was perched on the edge of the cushion, the three police officers sat back down, and Dancer said, 'I'm afraid I have some bad news for you, Mrs Goldstein.'

'He's dead, isn't he?' asked Judith Goldstein, her voice soft and well modulated.

Dancer grimaced. 'I'm afraid so.'

'What happened?'

'It's not very pleasant.'

'I didn't expect it to be. Tell me.'

Dancer didn't know what to say. He was sick inside at telling people how their loved ones had been horribly mutilated and killed by an unknown assassin. He looked desperately at Jane King who picked up his signal. 'This is the most difficult part of our job,' she said.

'Just tell me.'

'He has been cruelly treated.'

'Who by? Why?'

'We don't know.'

Just then Constable Gratton came in with a tray of tea things, and a whisky bottle and glasses. She put them on the table and said to Judith Goldstein. 'Have a cup of tea, love.'

'*Tea*. How can I drink tea with my husband dead, and no one will tell me what's happened to him?' She burst into tears.

Gratton went over, sat next to her and put her arm around the weeping woman. 'Don't cry,' she said. 'I know everything looks bad. But don't cry.'

'Everything *is* bad,' she sobbed.

Dancer looked at his two colleagues desperately.

'Can I see him?' asked Judith Goldstein.

This was the one question that Dancer dreaded above all others. 'I don't think it would be a good idea.'

'It might not be him.'

'It is.' He was emphatic.

'How do you know?'

'He was identified by certain physical characteristics.' He couldn't bring himself to tell her that it was his dental work.

'Like what?'

'Mrs Goldstein, please.' Jack Dancer had seen and heard and done most things in his twenty years as a copper. But there were some situations that had never become any easier since he was a young probationer who had had to break the news of a husband's death to his young widow. And although he didn't know it, that was the one thing that had kept him human, where so many of his fellow officers had turned into unfeeling automatons.

'What about his face?' Judith Goldstein looked from him to the others, as if seeking the answer to a question she couldn't bear to ask.

Christ, thought Jack Dancer, I'm making a right pig's ear of this. He just shook his head, and Judith Goldstein cried even harder.

A dreadful hush descended upon the room, broken

only by the muted sound of the woman's sobs, until it was shattered by the sound of the doorbell.

'I'll go,' said Jane King, and returned minutes later, followed by a middle-aged man carrying a leather bag. 'Doctor Harvey,' she said, and the man went to Judith Goldstein's side.

'I think you should go straight to bed,' he said to the young woman.

'I have to speak to these people,' protested Goldstein's wife.

'You can talk to them later,' said the doctor firmly, and gave Dancer, who he rightly surmised was in charge, a stern look. 'Right now, sleep is the best thing for you.'

29

After Mrs Goldstein had been led away protesting by the doctor, Dancer said to the three police officers, 'Sorry. I made a complete balls-up of that.'

'Impossible not to under the circumstances,' said Jane King. 'You did all right.'

'But we didn't get any information about who might want her husband dead.'

'We'll talk to her again later.'

'Constable,' said Dancer to Gratton. 'Are you staying here?'

'Until I'm relieved.'

'Well, try and talk to her, will you? And get whoever comes on next to do the same. But take it easy. I don't want to put the poor cow through an interrogation, but we've got to get this bloke, and someone must know something. Maybe it's her.'

He rubbed his fingers through his hair. 'Frankly, I'm at my wit's end. Come on you two, let's get back to the station and see what's new.'

They drove back to south London in silence, each preoccupied with their own thoughts, and went straight to Dancer's office where a pile of messages were waiting.

'Christ,' said Dancer as he started to go through them. 'Looks like the shit's really hitting the fan. Everyone wants to get in on the act now. I've been summoned to the Yard to have a chat with the big cheese on the fifth floor. I'm beginning to wish I'd never got involved in this mess.'

But Dancer didn't have an inkling of just how big a mess it was to become, as he drove himself to the Metropolitan Police headquarters, where he was ushered into the office of the assistant commissioner.

'Jack,' said the tired-looking uniformed man behind the big desk, who didn't bother to stand when Dancer entered the room.

'Sir.'

'Are you sure you're up to this?'

'Sir?'

'This torture business. You don't seem to be getting anywhere, and big questions are being asked. Special Branch want to come in on it, and even MI5. They've got bugger all to do these days.'

'Do you think they could do any better?'

'Let's face it, Jack, they couldn't do any worse.'

'Then good luck to them. All I've got to go on so far is sweet Fanny Adams. These people are being nicked off the street wholesale. There's no connection between them. No rhyme or reason to any of it, really. The only one that makes any sense is the bloke from Manchester. The bank manager. At least I can see why he was tortured. Or at least I think I can. He did a bunk with three quarters of a million quid in used banknotes. Now, that's a good enough reason for a lot of people to want him to spill the beans about what he'd done with it. But the others . . .' Jack Dancer shrugged. 'They must've had something that somebody wanted, but it beats me what it was. They ranged from the fairly well off to the seriously rich. Some of them worked and some of them didn't. There's not even a connection between the kind of jobs. For instance, one bloke was an advertising copywriter, another sold prestige motors, a third was a money broker in the city. A sensitive job, sure. Potentially a lot of cash involved. But nothing's come to light to show that he was at it.'

'Everybody's got secrets, Jack.'

'Sure. I appreciate that that's what it must all boil down to. But what kind of secrets? And how about the girl? Penelope Bannister. What secrets did she have? She was no more than a jumped-up clerk.'

'But presumably she had access to the computer bank where she worked?'

'But not for anything really interesting. She's been checked out, too. The price of fish, maybe. But that's about it.'

'So what about this Goldstein chap?'

'This one's turning into a nightmare. I've had Special

116

Branch treading on my toes as well. But try getting any useful information out of a semi-hysterical wife. Come on, sir. You've been there. And that's about all I'm dealing with on this case in the way of witnesses. Because there aren't any. All I've got are traumatized people who've seen, or not been allowed to see, their nearest and dearest seriously fucked up. It doesn't make for a good question and answer session. Whoever's doing this is the most cold-blooded and callous individual, or bunch of individuals, I've ever come up against.'

'And he or they have got to be stopped,' the AC said.

'Don't you think I know that?'

'Then get out there and get some results, Jack. You can have all the facilities you require. Extra troops, overtime, anything. But get a result, and make it fast, or you'll be off the case.'

'Yes, sir,' said Jack Dancer, and gathering the tatters of his professional reputation around him, he left.

30

The Great Beast roamed its underground lair on cloven hooves, sniffing at the tainted, sulphurous atmosphere. He looked up through the miles of dirt, conduit, concrete and buildings above him, and sensed that the gate of hell would soon open and allow the denizens of the lower world to play their infernal games with humanity. He made the rictus that was the closest he could come to a smile, and sensed that the time was near. The time of the serpent. The time of Armageddon. The day of destruction.

Mariella Newman felt him too. Through every nerve in her body she sensed him gathering his powers. But she was not afraid. She had power of her own, although it was being limited by her craven henchman, the Crow Man. Yet she was willing to bide her time. Constant practice had honed her talent, so that she was now much stronger than even the Crow Man appreciated. As a test, she concentrated hard, and two of the carrion who were sitting on the topmost branches of one of the trees in the square exploded into fragments of skin, bone, guts and feathers, and dripped down on to the flower beds below.

She smiled as she felt their pain and, in the split second that she destroyed them, she held the photograph of her husband and child tightly to her bosom, and dreamed of the day when she would destroy their torturer in the same way.

'Soon,' she crooned to herself. 'Soon come.'

Trace read about his latest exploits in the papers and smiled grimly. Little do they know, he thought, but couldn't work out where the thought had come from, and dismissed it. He'd checked his Swiss bank account, and the balance of the payment for the job on Goldstein had been deposited. The account was bursting with cash, but he rarely touched it. Money held little interest for him, except to pay for his expensive tastes in clothes and cars. But people loved to pay, and who was he to argue? The bloody fools. He could charge them anything he liked. And although he did not need the money, he was hungry for another commission. The blood lust was on him, and he shivered with pleasure as he thought of his most recent victims. Although he was not aware of it, the Great Beast's mind was melding with his, driving him to even more horrific acts. Trace went to the old factory in Peckham, which still stunk of Goldstein's seared body, and paced up and down the concrete floor urging the telephone to ring.

Jack Dancer returned to his office, turned his chair to look at the city that stretched away in front of him to the river and beyond, and considered his position.

He knew that he was between the devil and the deep blue sea, although he had no idea of the irony of that particular phrase.

On one hand, he was in charge of the biggest murder inquiry in the capital for several years, on the other hand, he had no idea of the identity of the perpetrator, who appeared to come and go like a will-o'-the-wisp. He had no witnesses, only the thinnest of motives, and no idea what to do next. His career was on the line and he knew it.

He turned back to his desk and began to go through the messages and faxes that lay deep upon it, like snow on a winter hillside. One in particular caught his eye. It was a telephone message, timed and dated for the previous afternoon.

It simply read: Follow the yellow brick road.

What the ..., he thought. Now some silly fucker's making jokes.

He didn't recognize the handwriting on the slip of paper, which had been torn from a police officer's notebook, and he was just about to consign the message to the wastepaper basket, when he thought better of it, folded it carefully and put it inside his wallet.

31

That night, Jack Dancer had the most vivid and terrifying dream of his life. One that seemed to last for hours and take on a life of its own.

He had long since stopped working regular shift hours, and if he had bothered to tot up his overtime entitlement, he would have been the richest officer in the Met. King and Evans had gone home hours before, leaving Dancer sitting at his desk in darkness, except for the pool of light from the goose-necked lamp that stood on one corner. He worked on the reports that his team had collated until he could hardly see straight. Finally he decided to call it a day, go home, and get some rest. It was midnight when he left the station, and he heard a distant clock strike the hour as he climbed wearily into his car. Dancer lived alone in a tiny flat over one of a row of shops in Nunhead. He put his car in its usual slot next to the big, wheeled garbage cans in the tiny parking area of the small supermarket on the corner of the parade, let himself in through the front door, which was actually at the back of the DIY shop he lived above, and went upstairs. Once there, he put on the kettle and poured himself his nightly allowance of a large Scotch, ice and water, and went into the living room. He kicked off his shoes, switched on the late movie on TV, and collapsed into an easy chair.

He sipped at the Scotch as he watched the old fifties western unravel its tired plot, until he heard the kettle click off and went to make a cup of tea and investigate the food situation. Inside the fridge he found a sausage pizza coming up to its sell-by date, and he slipped it into the oven whilst he put a teabag, milk and sugar into a china mug.

He sipped the brew whilst he waited for the pizza to warm through, then slid it on to a plate and took it back to the Scotch and the film.

He ate half the pizza before abandoning it, finished his drink, switched off the set, and went to bed.

He undressed completely, cleaned his teeth and climbed gratefully between the cool sheets that were all that was on the bed.

His last memory was the halo from the streetlight in the road outside, seen through the open curtains of his bedroom window, before he fell into a deep sleep.

When Dancer had been young, maybe nine or ten, his favourite uncle had taken him to see a rerun of *The Wizard of Oz* at their local cinema one Christmas Eve.

Dancer's father had died when he was three, and the young Jack had been brought up in a house full of women, so that a man's influence was welcome. His uncle had been the closest thing to a dad he'd ever known, before he killed himself some years later over money troubles.

That evening, a total and wonderful surprise for the boy, was one of his fondest recollections of childhood, and he still remembered how it had felt to sit in the most expensive seats in the balcony, with an ice cream and a bag of sweets, and the reassuring shape of his uncle sitting in the seat next to him.

And when the dream started that was exactly where he was. The tub of ice cream was cold in his hand, the cinema smelled exactly as it had that night, a mixture of warm air from the heating system, hot-dog sausages from the counter in the foyer, and his uncle's aftershave. Dancer smiled and leaned forward in anticipation as Dorothy and Toto flew over the rainbow to Munchkin land, and met the Good Witch and the Wicked Witch of the West, and were shown the Yellow Brick Road that led to the land of Oz.

And when Judy Garland, who Dancer had fallen madly in love with that night (although he didn't realize then that she was already grown up and almost at the end of her own personal yellow brick road), and her dog were about to start their journey to the Emerald City, he found himself with them, actually inside the screen, being waved off by the Munchkins.

He didn't feel at all out of place being there, and from the look on the face of Dorothy, she didn't seem to find it unusual either, as she and Jack Dancer linked hands and set off together.

But he noticed at the edge of the road, where the woods began, other faces appearing, with slavering mouths, sharp teeth and hungry red eyes that watched the travellers greedily. He tried to point them out, but the music was too loud, and their own movements too frenetic for Dorothy to notice.

The road narrowed and the branches of the trees, like

beckoning figures, closed above them. At last the music slowed and got quieter, and the run became a walk.

'Dorothy,' he said, realizing he was talking with the voice of a boy, and when he looked down he saw that his body was also that of a child, 'Dorothy. There are monsters watching us.'

'No,' she said, her red spangled shoes glistening in the evening light. 'No. You're imagining things.'

'I'm not, they're there. Look.'

But when he looked again, the monsters had vanished, and when he looked back, both the girl and her dog had vanished too. As the sun set over the hillside, the yellow road became dark and shadowy, and young Jack Dancer shivered as he stood alone. 'Dorothy, Toto,' he cried. But there was no reply.

The trees seemed to loom lower over the road. Dancer felt cold and lonely as he walked along the pavement into the oncoming darkness hoping to find his new friends. Then suddenly there was a flash of lightning and a crash of thunder and it began to rain.

The rain was hard and cold and the boy took shelter in the bole of one of the trees, its huge trunk sheltering him from the worst of the weather.

And then, strangely, in his dream he fell asleep. Only to dream again. Was it the first dream, or a dream within a dream? he wondered. Because all along he'd known he'd been sleeping in his own bedroom, but could do nothing about it.

In the second dream, the yellow of the road had turned red as the moon rose in a clear sky. Yet it was still raining. The water was the same scarlet as the eyes of the monsters he'd seen, and it gathered in pools on top of the bricks. Dancer held up his small boy's hand and saw that it was red too, and the water that dripped from his fingers was the colour of blood. But it was too thick and viscous to be water, and all of a sudden he knew that it *was* blood. With a cry he tried to wipe it off on the material of his trousers.

And the monsters themselves had returned. They peered at him through the wood, and although he wanted to run, he couldn't move.

He sat paralysed in the shelter of the tree as they came closer and closer still, until he could feel their rank breath on his face, and smell the disgusting stink that rose from their mangy bodies.

He tried to scream, but nothing came out of his mouth when he opened it, and although he wanted to flee he still could not move, no matter how hard he tried.

The closest monster was a huge behemoth with fangs as long as a man's index finger. Its eyes were as red as the moon that moved across the sky and the rain that kept falling. It reached out for Dancer, and he tried to scream again, putting all his energy into the effort, until with a start he woke up in his own bed, his body streaming with sweat in the still and hot night air.

He got out of bed and wiped himself with the damp sheet, then went to the kitchen and ran a glass full of cool water, which he swallowed in one gulp. He looked through the window down to the area at the back of the shops and realized that his dream was far from over. For there, in the red moonlight, the same monsters cavorted together, every few seconds looking up at his window with their strange scarlet eyes.

Jack Dancer had not known such fear in all his years

as a policeman, despite having been in dozens of life-threatening situations. But no matter how many dangerous men that, armed and unarmed, he had faced down, nothing had prepared him for what he saw as he stood in the calm of his own kitchen.

He dropped the glass into the sink, where it shattered into a thousand pieces, then turned and ran back to his bedroom. He pulled on his shirt and trousers, stuffed his feet into his shoes and crashed downstairs to the front door. He threw it open. The parking area was as empty and silent as when he had parked his car.

Thank God, he thought, as he leaned his head against the doorjamb. A hand snaked out from behind one of the garbage cans and fastened itself on to his shoulder.

Jack Dancer did scream then. A full-throttled, hysterical cry that echoed across the parking lot and bounced back from the brickwork of the surrounding buildings. It was a scream that should have woken the dead, but although at least a hundred people lived in the flats, not one light came on in any of the windows, and Jack Dancer was left to face whatever lurked in the darkness alone.

Dancer was lifted easily, as if his fifteen stone was nothing, and yanked into the even deeper shadows behind a bin that stunk of rotten meat. He just knew that thick white maggots squirmed in there, sucking the juices from the meat into their bloated bodies as they waited to turn into bluebottles and fly.

And then as the red moon moved across the sky its rays struck deep into the shadows, and Dancer saw exactly who or what he was up against. He felt his bowels void into his trousers, and another foul stink joined that of the garbage bins.

The thing was enormous. As tall as the bin itself, which was all of twelve feet high, and almost as wide. It was black as ink except for its long, white teeth that dripped thick saliva, and its eyes, which took the red from the moon and almost hypnotized Dancer as they stared into his.

The thing, whatever it was, opened its mouth, and Jack Dancer could see hundreds of fangs. He knew with complete certainty that if something didn't happen soon he was going to be a late-night snack for the monstrous being which held his shoulder so tightly he could feel the bones begin to shatter, when, with a flutter of wings, a pure white bird landed on the edge of the garbage bin, its feathers tipped with red from the moon.

The beast that held him heard the flutter of wings too, and turned its head away from Dancer in the direction of the bird, dropped the man out of its grip, and lunged at it. The beast's long arm caught the bird and tore its midsection from its body. *It's a dove*, thought Dancer, as he pushed himself out from behind the bins on his backside, feeling the coldness of his faeces on his upper thighs, and grimacing in disgust.

The beast turned back towards him, but suddenly the area at the back of the parade of shops was full of white birds, as if the hot summer night had turned into winter, and snow had begun to fall. They covered the beast in their feathery glow and smothered it. Dancer watched mesmerized as the huge black brute was borne down to the tarmac under the weight of the thousands of winged creatures, and suddenly he was back in his bed again, and the first rays of the rising sun were shining through the window in front of him. He had never been more glad to see daylight in his entire life.

He lay where he was, once more under the single sheet, and he felt down to the back of his naked legs, which were as clean as when he'd got into bed, and despite himself began to shake with relief.

He thought about the dream, or series of dreams, and climbed out of bed, walked back through the flat and checked the area where his car was parked. It was deserted except for the manager of the supermarket who was overseeing an early delivery of bread. There were no monsters, no white doves, dead or alive, and Dancer let out a shuddering sigh. Suddenly he thought of something, went to his suit jacket, took out his wallet and looked at the telephone message he had received the previous day.

The page from the police notebook, he now realized, was his own. He looked inside the notebook, and found a ragged edge that perfectly matched the torn-out piece he was holding, which was completely blank.

Christ, he thought to himself, I'm going mad.

32

Dancer held the piece of paper for what seemed like a lifetime before dropping it to the floor and going back to the bedroom. He examined his trousers, which were clean and unfouled, and went for a shower and shave.

Afterwards he dressed in a clean shirt, pants and socks, put on his suit and shoes, tied his tie and went to make a cup of tea.

As he filled the kettle he saw that broken glass littered the bottom of the sink and had to put his hand on the draining board for support. Christ, he thought, confused. Could any of that dream last night be true?

He made his tea and ate a slice of dry toast standing up, looking through the kitchen window, before going out, getting into his car and going back to the station.

Jane King, who was already at the desk she was reluctantly sharing with Evans, looked up as Dancer walked through the door. 'Bloody hell!' she said. 'What's the matter with you? You look like you've seen a ghost.'

'Maybe I have,' replied Dancer. 'Any chance of a coffee.'

'Sure.' She got up, and went to the table that supported their meagre refreshment supplies and an electric kettle.

'Can I ask you something, Jane?' said Dancer.

'Sure. As long as it's not for money. I'm a bit short this month, and it's a long time till payday.'

'No. It's nothing like that. I just wondered if you'd been having any strange dreams lately.'

She looked over at him as she spooned instant coffee into a mug. 'No. I don't think so, sir. Why?'

'No reason. I had a real weird one last night. That's all. I think this case is getting to me.'

'I'm not surprised. It's enough to get to anybody. What kind of dream?'

'It was about Judy Garland. I was in the land of Oz.'

'A bit like working here, I should think.'

'You're not wrong. Then I woke up, but I wasn't really awake. At least I don't think so. And I met a monster.'

'I meet them all the time. Usually on Friday nights in the pub about closing time.'

Dancer smiled.

'Does the dream worry you?' asked King.

'Not really. Except I don't usually remember them. Not much past getting up anyway. But this one is sticking around.'

'I'd be careful if I were you, sir. Otherwise the super'll have you up in front of a shrink.'

'That thought had crossed my mind,' said Dancer, as he touched his left shoulder, which was giving him some pain. When he'd been in the shower, he'd noticed it was heavily bruised, as if it had been gripped by a powerful hand.

33

And now, although only a few were aware of it, things started to move faster in the grim scenario that was being played out above and beneath the sordid streets of south London.

The Great Beast wandered from one end of his lair to the other, cursing under his breath in a language that was as old as time itself. He was angry and frustrated. The dream demon he had sent to Dancer the night before had been thwarted by some other entity. Another powerful force had stepped on to the stage, ready to play its part in the drama. 'Damn them,' the Great Beast raged. 'Damn them if they would dare interfere with my plan. I will succeed if I have to destroy the whole planet to do it. And I will begin *now*!'

At the old factory in Peckham the phone rang.

Trace picked up the receiver on the second ring. 'Yellow,' a voice said, and if Trace noticed that the voice was fractionally different from the usual contact, he ignored the fact.

'Yes.'

'You're wanted.'

'Yes.'

'Euston. Four. One-o-eight.' And the receiver was put down.

Trace picked up his jacket and went out to the Cosworth, locking up behind him as he went, and pointed the car north.

He drove to the Euston station NCP, went down to the fourth level, parked the Ford where he could, and walked to parking bay 108, pulling on a pair of thin leather gloves as he went. In the space was parked a Mercedes estate. He took the key from where it had been hidden on the top of the rear offside tyre and opened up the car. He switched on the ignition and turned on the stereo. There was a tape in the slot and when he pressed Play, an anonymous male voice said:

'*Your target is Stephen Collier. Full details in the usual place. His wife is pregnant. She's the lever. He has information about a computer system we need to access soonest. Please confirm acceptance.*'

After that there was only the hiss of magnetic particles on the blank tape.

Trace ejected the cassette and put it in his jacket pocket, then reached over and pulled up the carpet in the well on the passenger side of the car. There was an A4 sized envelope lying there. He folded it in two and put it into his pocket, pushed the carpet flat and left the car, relocking the door and replacing the key where he'd found it. The whole exercise took less than five minutes.

He went back to the Ford, took off his gloves and drove out of the car park and to another of his safe addresses, a small but luxurious flat in a purpose-built block in Streatham.

Once there, he opened one of the three cans of Sapparo that were the only contents of the fridge, went into the bright living room that looked out over the common, sat on the sofa, and took a sip before opening the envelope.

Inside were several candid photographs of a man and woman captured as they went about their daily business, obviously unaware of the photographer. Stephen Collier was about thirty-five, tall, slim and dark. The woman was some years younger, blonde, attractive, and obviously heavily pregnant. With the photographs were details of their home address, a flat in Putney, his work address, which was a computer company in Middlesex, and the respective phone numbers, plus the number and description of their car.

On a separate sheet were their personal vital statistics, and other information about their credit worthiness, taste in books and films, and more personal details than Trace could ever need or want.

Finally there was a number to call to accept or reject the job, and details of the fee.

It was Trace's biggest yet, and almost caused him to blink.

He went into the bedroom, found another illegal mobile phone and called the number.

A voice which sounded like the one on the tape in his pocket answered after half a dozen rings.

'Yes,' the voice said.

'Yellow,' said Trace. 'Accepted. You know the terms.'

'Ten per cent out front.'

'Correct.'

'Done.'

'What do you want to know?'

'Project Omega. Everything.'

'He'll know what I'm talking about?'

'He'll know.'

'I'll begin as soon as the first instalment's in the bank.'

'It'll be there within the hour. This number is live on a twenty-four-hour basis.'

'A pleasure doing business with you,' said Trace, and hung up.

He went to the window and stared out across the dusty green grass to the tree line, where every branch seemed to support the weight of dozens of crows.

34

Mariella Newman was aware that momentous events were beginning to happen, and she knew that the birds that scratched and clattered above her at night were aware too.

She went upstairs to the attic, where the Crow Man lounged in his usual place on the sofa amongst a phalanx of black birds, and said, 'What exactly is going on?'

'The final chapter is about to be written,' replied the Crow Man sucking on the remains of a particularly juicy chicken bone that one of his winged friends had rescued from a discarded box, before adding it to the growing pile that was heaped on the floor next to the arm of the chair.

'How does it feel to eat your relatives?' asked the woman, her lips curling in disgust.

'Those stupid birds are no relatives of ours,' replied the Crow Man haughtily.

'And aren't you ever going to clean this place up? It's beginning to stink.'

'Then it will match your quarters downstairs,' said the Crow Man.

Mariella Newman looked at him through slitted eyes and snapped, 'Don't dare criticize me, or you'll wish that you'd never left the egg. I'm not happy with your behaviour at all, and it would take little for me to see you and the rest of your mangy crew cooked and served up by Colonel Sanders too.'

The Crow Man gave her a look which was a mixture of hatred and fear, and the crows flapped their wings and cawed in displeasure, but Mariella silenced them with a glance. 'So tell me,' she demanded. 'Before I sacrifice some of your feathered friends. I can do it, you know. Don't tempt me to demonstrate.'

The Crow Man gathered the last of his dignity around him and said, 'The battle lines are being drawn for a mighty conflict which will seal the fate of all mankind. Trace is involved. Heavily involved. He is the tool that the Great Beast is using.'

'I don't care about this Beast of yours. I fear nothing on this world or any other. My life ended long ago. But Trace is about to inflict more misery. That I cannot bear. I want him dead, and I want him dead today. Now. But before he dies and goes to hell, I want him to suffer some of the torment that he has caused others. Just a little to give him the taste of what I have had to swallow since my husband and child were murdered.'

'No, mistress,' said the Crow Man. 'I cannot. Will not. Not yet.'

'*No!*' screamed Mariella Newman. '*No. You* dare to deny *me*?' Her body seemed to grow bigger as she screamed, her arms, legs and neck extended, until her head almost seemed to touch the ceiling, and as she cast her gaze around the room, one by one, as if hit by high-powered bullets, crows' heads began to explode in a spray of flesh, blood, bone and brains.

'No, mistress, please,' the Crow Man pleaded. 'Do not kill any more. They are my friends.'

'Then will you do as I say?'

After a moment the Crow Man said, 'I will try. But the powers of the Great Beast are stronger than mine, and he may defeat me.'

'Then God help you,' said Mariella Newman. 'Because believe me, he'll be the only one who can.'

35

But the Crow Man, with all his mighty powers, could not destroy Trace. Nor could Mariella Newman. A higher power was at work on the Torturer's fate, and no matter how the woman ranted and raved and railed at her servant, no matter how many crows she destroyed, until their bodies piled up in the attic and the place stank of death, she could not kill the man she most hated in the world.

She spun and danced, making the birds spin and dance in their turn until she exploded them like fleshy fire-crackers until the walls and ceiling of the attic hung with meat, and she and the Crow Man were soaked with blood. When the death toll of birds was in the hundreds, and the Crow Man's white face was even paler with fear and anger, she knelt on the splintery floor of the attic amidst the carnage, and wept and beat her breast. Then the Crow Man said, 'It is ordained, mistress. There is nothing we can do to change what is ordained.'

Mariella lifted her ravaged face and fixed him with a glare that chilled his flesh to the bone. 'You will regret the day you said that to me,' she spat. 'For I will never rest until he is destroyed. And if you go with him, that too will be ordained, you piece of dung.'

*

When Trace got the confirmation that the money had been paid, he started to shadow Stephen Collier and his wife. It was the easiest job he had ever done. Collier came and went every weekday as regularly as clockwork, leaving his wife at home. She would go shopping every morning at ten precisely, driving down to the local supermarket and picking up a few purchases. Apart from that she stayed close to home, waiting for her husband's return at six each evening, after which they battened down the hatches until bedtime at about eleven, when the lights in the flat went off. There was no need for any fancy surveillance equipment or bugs for Trace to interface with their lifestyle.

Three days after he'd accepted the job, Trace pounced.

He dressed that morning in the uniform of a paramedic, after checking that the Volvo ambulance he'd stolen many months before, and changed the plates of, was running smoothly.

At nine o'clock in the morning he drove the ambulance out of the factory gates and headed towards Putney.

At five past ten he was parked by the supermarket entrance, saw Collier's wife turn into the car park, then followed.

At that time of day, during the week, the parking lot was almost empty, and Diana Collier parked close to the back entrance. Trace stopped the ambulance so that it not only blocked her car in, but hid it from the sight of anyone not on either side of her vehicle. There was no one.

Trace hopped out of the driver's door of the ambulance as Diana Collier slowly exited from her car, weighed down with the baby in her womb.

Trace smiled his most charming smile at her. She smiled in return and said, 'I don't think I need you today. At least I hope not.'

Trace kept smiling as he approached the woman. 'How long?' he asked.

'About another two months.'

'Don't bet on it,' said Trace as he glanced round quickly, saw that they were alone, and punched the woman viciously between the eyes, then caught her as she fell.

He held her easily with one arm and half-dragged, half-supported her round to the back of the ambulance and opened the door.

An elderly woman came out of the back entrance of the market and looked askance at the scene.

'Nothing to worry about, love,' said Trace reassuringly in an Irish accent. 'She's just had a dizzy spell.'

'Will she be all right?' asked the woman, noting Diana Collier's advanced condition.

'As right as rain,' said Trace. 'We're just taking her to the hospital. Can't be too careful, you know.'

'No you can't,' said the woman. 'Take care of her, won't you?'

'Course. Now I'd better be getting on,' and he pulled Diana Collier up into the back of the ambulance and let the door swing closed.

Quickly, he dropped the woman on to the stretcher bed and secured the straps around her body, then plugged an IV containing a weak anaesthetic into her arm. He checked her pulse, then jumped out of the back, slammed the door and locked it, and went back to the cab.

Once inside, he started the engine, pulled out of the car park, switched on the blue light on top of the Volvo, and rapidly negotiated the journey back to Peckham.

36

The crows watched it all and chattered to themselves as they followed the ambulance's route, and saw Trace drive into the compound of the old factory and lock the gates behind him.

He opened the back doors of the Volvo and looked at the woman. She was awake by then, but still groggy from the anaesthetic and the punch that had raised bruises on both eyes. She looked back at him with such fear that only the hardest hearted of men would have ignored it.

Trace was that man.

He pulled out the wheeled gurney she was lying on and pushed her into the factory and on to the waiting plastic sheet, positioning the gurney precisely in the middle.

Then he stripped off the paramedic's uniform and pulled on some ancient Levi's and a flannel shirt.

All the time the woman watched him, but made not one sound.

When he was ready, Trace took out one of his mobile phones and tapped in Collier's number at work. He got the switchboard, and asked to be put through. Collier answered on the second ring. 'Stephen Collier,' he said.

'I have your wife,' said Trace without preamble.

'What?' The connection was not good, and Trace could hear a myriad of other voices, other lives in the background.

'Your wife,' he repeated. 'I have her with me.'

'What are you talking about?'

'If you listened, you'd know,' said Trace, irritably. 'Mother and baby doing fine. So far. Do you want to speak to her?'

'If this is a joke, it's not funny.'

'This is no joke, believe me. Treat it as one and you'll be sorry.'

'Who *are* you?'

'Wouldn't you like to know? Just for now I'm your worst nightmare. The man who has your wife and unborn child. Isn't that enough?'

'What do you want?'

'I want you to go home now. Don't speak to anyone about what I've said. Just tell them you don't feel well. I'll give you an hour, then ring you there.'

There was a pause. 'I can't just walk out.'

'Yes you can. Speak to your wife. She'll tell you.'

Trace placed the phone on the edge of the gurney and looked down at Diana Collier. 'You heard what I said. I have your husband on the phone. Talk to him. Tell him to do what I said. Exactly what I told him and no more, and I'll take you back home. Otherwise ...' He didn't finish the sentence. 'Do you understand?' he asked.

'My baby,' she said. 'Don't hurt my baby.'

'That'll be up to your husband. Just make sure he

139

does what I tell him, and everything will be OK. All right?'

She nodded, and he could see the beads of sweat on her face.

'Good,' he said, then picked up the phone and held it to her face.

'Steve,' she said, her voice rusty. She swallowed hard. 'Do what he says. Do anything.'

Trace heard Collier's voice come through the earpiece in reply. 'Steve. Just do it,' said Diana Collier. 'He's mad.' She looked up at Trace, her face fearful at what she'd said, but he didn't respond. 'Please, Steve. Nothing can be worth hurting our baby.'

Trace put the phone back to his own ear.

'Are you all right . . .' he heard Collier say.

'She's fine,' said Trace. 'Now go home. I'll call you again in an hour. And remember. Don't tell anyone, especially the police. It will be worse for Diana and Junior if you do.' And he killed the connection.

'What is it you want?' asked Diana Collier. 'We have nothing. No money. This must be a mistake.'

'No mistake,' said Trace. 'Your husband has something I need.'

'But what? Please tell me.'

Trace shook his head. 'You'll find out soon enough,' he said, and looked at his watch. 'In about fifty-seven minutes in fact. How does your face feel?'

'Sore.'

'Do you want me to dress it? It's not cut. I'm sorry I had to do that.'

She shook her head. 'Leave it,' she said. 'Just don't hurt my baby.'

'That'll be your husband's decision.'

'I wish you'd stop saying that. And I need to go to the loo.'

'Sure,' said Trace. 'I don't want to make this any more uncomfortable than it has to be. But no tricks.'

The woman nodded, and Trace unstrapped her, helped her off the gurney and into the toilet. He stood outside whilst she urinated, then took her back, and sat her on one of the chairs dotted about the room. 'You can sit here for now,' he said. 'Do you fancy some music while we're waiting?'

She looked at him amazed.

'It makes the time go faster.'

'If you want.'

'Anything in particular?'

'I can't think.'

'You look like a Simply Red fan to me. Are you?'

'I don't know.'

'You must know.'

'I'm sorry.'

'Mick Hucknall. The one with all the red curly hair.'

'I've seen him on TV, I think.'

'Do you like him?'

'I've never thought.'

'What was the last record you bought?'

'I can't remember.'

'Course you can.'

'Stravinsky.'

'You like classical music?'

'Yes.'

'I prefer something with a bit more bass myself.'

'Like what?'

141

'Led Zeppelin. *Four Symbols*. Now that's an album.'

'I don't understand. What do you mean, four symbols?'

'Each member of the band is represented by a symbol. Runes. Black magic, maybe. The band were supposed to be into that at one time. Bad things happened to them.' Led Zeppelin's was the only music Trace could bear to listen to. In it he sensed some of the same feelings as his own.

'I've never heard it.'

'Would you like to?'

'If you want.'

'I want.'

Trace went over to the workbench and pulled a cloth off the JVC micro-system that stood there. 'Excellent stereo,' he said. 'Four speakers, surround sound. Just listen to this.'

He switched on the stereo and pressed the CD Play button. The album was already in the player, and from all around the factory the opening bars of 'Black Dog' burst through the speakers.

Trace turned the volume up until the music seemed to be the only sound in the world, and he turned and walked back to Diana Collier.

The music was so loud that they could communicate only by looks, and for the first time Trace felt pity for the woman. He knew that whatever happened she would not leave the factory alive. He had not worn a mask or any disguise. She had seen him. And that was her death certificate. Signed, sealed, and notarized by his own hand.

He looked down and smiled at her tenderly, and terrified though she was, she smiled back.

37

Trace allowed the album to play through to its climax, then he looked at his watch. 'Not long now,' he said.

Exactly an hour after he had last spoken to Stephen Collier, he switched on his phone again and punched out the Colliers' home number. The receiver was snatched up after one ring. 'What have you done to her?' said Collier.

'What? No one home?' said Trace coolly.

'You know very well.'

'I hope you didn't make a fuss at work.'

'I said I had a bad stomach.'

'Good. No police?'

'Of course not. How is Diana?'

'In the pink.'

'You heartless bastard,' said Collier.

'Flattery will get you nowhere.'

'If you hurt her, I'll kill—'

'And nor will threats,' said Trace, with an edge of anger to his voice. 'Only one thing will.'

'What?'

'Tell me everything you know about the Omega Project.'

'*What?* Who are you?'

'That's of no consequence.'

'What do you know about Omega?'

'Nothing. That's why I need you to tell me all about it.'

'That's impossible. You don't understand. It's a Government contract out for tender. I had to sign the Official Secrets Act—'

'That's your problem.'

'I could go to prison—'

'Once again, your problem. But your biggest problem at the moment is that I'm holding your wife and unborn child here. It's not a pleasant place, and unless you tell me everything you know, I will be forced to do unpleasant things to her which would have serious repercussions on the baby. What's it to be by the way?'

Collier ignored the mocking question and simply said, 'Please don't.'

'Then tell me what I want to know. It's simple. Your knowledge in exchange for their health. I would've thought it was no contest. No one will know that you've told me.'

Which was an outright lie, but being lied to was not the worst thing that would happen to Stephen Collier that day.

'I can't,' said the man, almost tearfully.

'No such word. Speak to your wife. I'm sure she'll convince you.'

Trace walked over to where Diana Collier was sitting and handed her the phone. 'Tell him,' he said coldly. 'Tell him that I mean what I say. And be convincing.'

'Steve,' she said into the instrument, her voice cracking with fear and apprehension. 'Tell him what he wants to know. Everything. Anything. I'm in this horrible place. It stinks of death. Please. You must help me—'

Trace snatched the phone out of her hand. 'Listen, Steve, and listen well. You are going to do it. I promise you. Sooner or later, and with more or less pain to Diana. That's up to you. I'll give you an hour to think about it. I'll call you back there. And remember, this is our little secret, or it'll be the worse for Diana.'

He cut Collier off before he could speak again, put the phone back on to the bench and walked to one of the dirty windows that looked out over the factory yard. In the gaps between the buildings around him, he could see clouds beginning to gather. They were the colour of cigarette ash, and as they roiled together he heard the first rumblings of thunder in the distance, and felt the air around him become charged with electricity.

That summer storm was to be the fiercest in London since records began, and was all the worse for being totally unexpected. The meteorological report that morning had been similar to the ones every morning for a month. Hot, dry and still. The longest spell of above-average temperatures for the month of July for twenty years.

Thus it was as much a surprise in the Met Office as it was anywhere when the storm blew up on their computer screens from nowhere, and they were left as shocked as the rest of the population when it wreaked havoc from one end of the city to the other over the period of a few hours.

So London had gone to work in shirtsleeves and summer dresses that day. Windows had been left open despite the possibility of burglary, convertibles were left parked with their tops down, and twenty-seven healthy people woke up that morning unaware that it was to be their last day on earth.

Trace watched the storm gather from ground level, but Dancer, Evans and King were on the top floor of the police station and had a much better view of its genesis.

They were all in Dancer's office having their usual morning meeting, discussing the case, drinking innumerable cups of coffee and smoking, with the windows cracked open to allow in some semblance of fresh air, when they first felt a faint breeze from the south which quickly strengthened to a more substantial zephyr, disturbing the papers on Dancer's desk.

'What's going on?' he said, placing an ashtray to act as a paperweight.

'Looks like rain,' said Evans, as the sky began to darken.

'Not today,' said Jane King. 'I listened to the news on the way in, and they said it was going to be hot and dry again.' She adjusted one of the straps of her bra through her shirt, where the line of sweat that had collected under it was making her itch.

'Looks like they got it wrong, then,' said Evans, as he got to his feet and went over to the window that faced south. 'It's as black as pitch over there.'

He glanced down into the street below, where the detritus of a month of long, hot, dry and windless days began to dance down the street as the wind picked it up. Sweet wrappers, cigarette packets and old newspapers grown brittle and brown under the relentless rays of sun were all whisked along the pavement in a fine cloud of dust. Pedestrians were shielding their eyes.

The sky continued to darken as the sun disappeared behind the first tendrils of cloud that sped northwards across the city. King walked over to the door and switched on the overhead lights, before she and Dancer joined Evans at the window and watched as other lights in the surrounding offices and homes came on too.

The cloud thickened as it raced across the sky, until it was so dark outside that people on the ground could hardly see to the end of the street before the orange sodium lamps, hung high on their giraffe-necked poles, clicked on as their light sensors detected a false evening. King shivered as the temperature dropped to below seventy for the first time in a month.

Then, without warning, came the first sheet of lightning, like a giant flash bulb that bleached everything bone white as it snapped the city in its single strobe.

The trio instinctively flinched as the white light filled the room. 'Christ,' said Evans. 'Did you see that?'

'You couldn't miss it, could you?' replied Jane King, but her words were drowned by a clap of thunder so loud that it felt as if the planet itself was splitting open.

In the aftermath of the crash, they heard the sound of breaking glass from outside, and later, Dancer swore that he saw the panes in the windows bulge as if they were going to implode and shower them with razor-sharp shards of glass.

'Move back,' he yelled. 'Get away from the windows. They might blow. This is no normal storm. It's like a bloody hurricane out there.'

As if to confirm his words, the rain came: not so much

147

a cloudburst as a constant downpour that flooded sewers and half the roads in the metropolitan area within minutes.

It was then that they heard the first sirens.

'Fire engines,' said Evans. 'This must've hit further south a few minutes ago. There'll be a few basements'll want pumping out.'

'Should we be doing something, Guv?' said Jane King.

'Like what?' said Dancer. 'We're CID, not uniform.'

'It's going to get pretty stretched downstairs soon,' said Evans. 'Maybe we should go and see if we can do anything to help.'

'If you want,' said Dancer, as another sheet of lightning flared in the sky, and the lights in the room flickered. 'Me, I'm going to stay up here and watch the show.'

Also watching the show was Mariella Newman. The first inkling she had of the storm's arrival was when she heard the alarmed crows cawing in the attic. She went upstairs, blanching as she entered the attic at the stench of decay that came from the bodies of the birds she'd destroyed. The Crow Man had made no move to clear them away, as if by leaving them there they were somehow still alive.

'Aren't you going to do anything about that smell?' she asked, as his tall figure paced the floorboards. 'And what's the matter with them?' She gestured at the living birds.

'Something's happening,' he said. 'It is beginning.'

'What?'

'The killing of the child.'

'What child?' she said, and the same terrible mixture

148

of hate and guilt that she'd felt on hearing of other victims of the Torturer, which perhaps she could have saved by talking to the authorities, began to fill her chest again. It was difficult for her to breathe, and the room took on a scarlet hue. But this time it was worse. A child. Just like her own.

'A very special one. This is Trace's destiny. And the child's, and ours. It will not be long now.'

'I want it stopped.'

'You do not have the power, mistress. Nor do I. Maybe no one has.'

'What is happening?' she asked as the dim light in the attic grew even dimmer, and the birds' movements became more agitated and their cries louder.

'A storm is brewing,' said the Crow Man. 'Like no storm seen here ever before. Who sent it, I have no idea. But it is the backdrop to momentous events.'

With a few words in a strange language he tried to calm the birds, but they paid him no heed.

As the first flash of lightning rent the skies, they put their heads underneath their wings, and beat their feet in a tattoo on the floor.

Trace fastened Diana Collier's arms and legs to the chair where she was sitting, and went upstairs to watch the rain lash the streets, and the thunder and lightning combine to make a visual and aural display that he had never seen the like of in all his life.

The water poured from the sky in grey rods that bounced back up two feet into the air, and the occasional car that passed the factory crept along at a snail's pace, main beams on, wipers hardly able to deal with the rain, even at double speed.

Hundreds of feet below where Trace stood, the Great Beast watched the storm through the eyes of the imps that had climbed up to view the carnage from the drains, even though they risked drowning as they did so.

But the Great Beast cared little if one imp survived the day, or one human being, with the exception of Matt Trace, who was doing the devil's own work for him.

38

Twenty-seven people perished in the few hours that the storm raged. Another four hundred and twenty people sustained injuries ranging from the very minor to full amputation, and the cost to the insurance companies for damage was estimated to be close to a billion pounds.

There were no murders and no suicides. People were too busy with other things to kill themselves or one another.

King and Evans helped out in the CAD room at Peckham Police Station, until the telephone lines over-loaded and communication was broken. After that they kept in touch with the outside world by radio, as the police in the street reported the damage to lives and property.

Dancer was as good as his word and stayed in his office, smoking and watching the pyrotechnics outside.

Thirty minutes into the storm, the power in the station failed and emergency generators came into action.

Mariella Newman went back downstairs in her house. Although she hated to admit it, the crows in the attic worried her, and despite being three floors below them she felt that she could still hear the sound of their bony feet beating on the ceiling.

The Great Beast rolled on the floor with satisfaction as he heard of the death and injury toll. Disasters were meat and drink to him, and with the news of each fresh casualty, the blood coursed faster through his veins.

Matt Trace watched amazed for exactly an hour, then went back downstairs and called Stephen Collier. But the phone in Putney was out of order. Trace cursed and smashed his portable on to the concrete floor. 'You've been reprieved,' he spat at Diana Collier.

39

The storm evaporated as quickly as it had arrived, and the clouds dispersed to allow the sun free reign once more over London. The whole town steamed like a wet cat in front of an electric fire.

Evans and King rejoined Dancer to look out over the city, which was covered in a damp fog.

'Jesus Christ,' said Evans, lighting a cigarette. 'Have you ever in your whole life seen anything like that?'

'No,' said Dancer. 'I never have.'

'It's chaos out there,' said Jane King. 'We nearly lost

control. There's been a whole lot of reports of looting coming in over the radio.'

'What did you expect?' said Dancer cynically. 'Public spiritedness.'

'There's been that as well,' said King. 'Rather more than we thought, to tell you the truth.'

'The Met Office's name's mud,' said Evans. 'If you'll excuse the pun. They had no idea this was going to happen.'

'Rather like October eighty-seven,' said Dancer. 'Remember that one?'

'I heard that the river overflowed in Vauxhall,' said King.

'Want to take a look round the town?' asked Dancer. 'See what the water's washed up?'

'Why not?' replied Evans. 'The phones are still out here. So we might as well.'

The phones were still out in Putney too. When Trace calmed down, he found another portable and tried the number every few minutes, spending the time between calls looking out at the storm until it died.

For another hour after the rain had stopped, and the city sweltered under the sun again, Trace kept pushing the redial button on the phone. After maybe a hundred tries and a hundred unobtainable signals, he finally heard the ringing tone in his ear and smiled.

But no one answered. Trace let it ring on and on for what seemed like hours until he killed the connection. He turned and looked at Diana Collier. 'Is your husband stupid?' he asked. 'He's not answering.'

She shook her head but didn't speak, and Trace tried

the number again. Still no answer, and he cursed in anger and frustration. He was used to the people in his power doing what he demanded of them, and he was not pleased.

He kept trying for another three hours, getting angrier and angrier as the time went by, and the fog that covered London settled like a damp blanket over Peckham. Every surface in the factory ran with moisture.

He considered going to the Colliers' house himself to find out what was going on, but dismissed the thought. He didn't want to leave the woman alone, but he didn't want to travel through the streets with her either. He caught several news bulletins on the radio, and by the sound of it, the road conditions were so bad that even a fairly short journey could take hours, so instead he stayed where he was, the anger and frustration he felt growing in his mind.

Eventually, around four in the afternoon, the phone was finally answered. It was picked up after the fourth ring and a voice that he didn't recognize reeled off the number he was calling.

Trace didn't know what was going on. Had the dumb fuck called in the police? There was no way of tracing the call even if he had. And would they be stupid enough to answer the phone themselves.

'Is Stephen Collier there?' he asked, his voice almost hesitant.

'He's not available at the moment. Who's calling?'

Trace ignored the question and instead said, 'Who am I speaking with?'

'Chief Officer McPherson, Putney Fire Station.'

'Is something wrong?'

'Are you a member of the family, sir?'

'No. A friend.'

'I'm afraid I have some bad news.'

Trace was silent and let the man talk on, but his brain was seething.

'You're obviously aware of the storm we had here today,' the fireman said. 'And I'm afraid Mr Collier was one of the casualties.'

'What happened?'

'A neighbour said he seemed to be in some distress. Something about his wife. Mr Collier went out into the street and was hit by some falling debris. He was dead on arrival at the hospital. No one could raise Mrs Collier, and as there's been some extensive flooding in the area; we were in the next street when we were asked to break in. I'm sorry to have to break the news to you, but Mrs Collier isn't in the building. I don't suppose you know—'

'No,' said Trace, trying to get a handle on the news and its implications. 'This is terrible. I'm sorry, I'll have to go.' And he pressed the kill button on the phone.

'Shit,' he said as he turned to Diana Collier, who was looking at him wide eyed. 'Bad news. Hubby's gone to Jesus. Which leaves us in a bit of a spot.'

For a split second the woman didn't know whether to believe him or not, but then the last words he had said on the phone flashed through her mind, and she realized what he was saying. As the truth hit her, her face contorted into a mask and she screamed. A sound like no other Trace had ever heard, and he had heard plenty. It echoed around the rafters of the building, and for the first time he was worried that someone outside the factory might hear, so with one stride he was beside her, and gave her a vicious rabbit punch to the back of her neck that knocked her clean off her chair and on to the damp concrete floor.

She lay very still. He kicked her hard in the ribs. She moaned and stirred, and he fetched some water from the bench and tossed it into her face. 'Wake up, you fucking bitch,' he said. 'We've got things to do.'

He dragged her over to a similar table to that on which he'd tortured Penelope Bannister, and which he'd got ready earlier, then lifted her on to it. She kept moaning as he did it, and when she was strapped securely in he slapped her face hard. She opened her eyes and looked directly at him, then spat into his face.

40

Dancer, Evans and King spent hours driving through the streets of south London in their unmarked police car that afternoon, marvelling at the damage the storm had wrought.

The river had overflowed at Vauxhall, and the closing of the Thames Barrier had not helped. In fact it had probably hindered, if anything, as most of the water had come downstream. The Albert Embankment was impassable, and firefighters and office staff could do nothing but look on helplessly as the basements of the St Thomas's Hospital buildings that faced the Houses of Parliament were flooded.

'Hell of a business,' said Dancer, not for the first time, as Evans had chivvied the car through traffic jam after traffic jam, past ROAD CLOSED signs, and pulled into the side of the road to allow public service vehicles with lights flashing and sirens wailing to pass.

'Where did it all come from?' asked Jane King. 'All that water.'

'Christ knows,' said Dancer. 'But we certainly copped it.'

'There's a lot of casualties,' said Evans, who had been monitoring the police radio that whispered from the dashboard of the car.

'Maybe our man's one of them,' said King hopefully.

'That's wishful thinking, Jane,' said Dancer. 'People like that never die when you want them to. They've got the luck of the bloody devil.'

And the devil was indeed with Trace that afternoon, although as yet Trace was not aware of it.

But others were, and as he started his most heinous task to date, a pair of bedraggled crows, who had been forced to take shelter as the storm raged, sat on one of the windowsills outside the factory and watched him at his terrible task.

He began by cutting the woman's clothes off. She was wearing a maternity dress that buttoned down the front, over a white cotton bra and matching knickers. It had been too hot for tights that morning, so Diana Collier had skipped wearing them.

After she had spat in his face, Trace had gagged her with gaffer tape, so all she could do was look at him as he stripped the clothes from her body.

When she was naked, the swell of her belly huge, white and vulnerable, he looked down at her. 'That stupid bastard of a husband of yours has cost me a fortune,' he said. 'Why did he have to go and get himself killed? He could just've told me what I wanted to know and everything would've been fine. So, Diana, I'm afraid you're going to be the one to pay. You and the brat inside you.'

This time Trace dispensed with the rubber gloves. This was personal, and he wanted to feel the blood and raw flesh between his fingers; taste her pain along with her bodily fluids. It was no longer business, it was pleasure.

He unfastened one of her hands and put it to his lips. The skin tasted salty and unclean in Trace's mouth, and he grimaced before biting the first joint of the little finger clean off, with a sound like a biscuit being broken.

She tore her hand from his grip, arched her back off the examination table, and rolled her head from side to side as she tried to scream, but could not because of the gag. Her face reddened with the exertion and she urinated and defecated violently from the pain.

Trace smiled as he spat out the finger tip and a mouthful of her blood.

'Tasted good,' he said as he wiped his mouth with the back of his hand.

He caught her arm again and retied it, then sluiced her mess on to the floor with more water, before walking around her naked body, examining it from all angles, his brow furrowed with concentration.

'Right,' he said, his lips and chin still red with gore. 'Let's get down to the serious business of the day.'

41

But the really serious business of the day had started before time had even properly begun, and only now was it coming to its culmination.

Because, as Trace was looking at Diana Collier with nothing but hatred in his heart, another storm was brewing between good and evil, of which he was totally unaware.

The two crows that were watching Trace sensed it first. Their feathers lifted as they felt the presence of other, even more powerful flocks of birds, and they huddled together in fear, but never once thought of leaving their perch, for they had been ordered to observe and report everything to their master, the Crow Man.

High above London a phalanx of hawks turned and wheeled when, from the south, a flock of white doves flew towards them.

There were thousands of birds in all; enough to show up on air traffic control computers at Heathrow and Gatwick, and to throw the controllers into a panic – as if a couple of squadrons of Sadam Hussein's MIGs had suddenly appeared over the Metropolis.

The two flocks met above Peckham just over the factory, and something like a Battle of Britain dogfight ensued.

Feathers flew as the birds pecked and clawed at each other, twisting and turning in the air, diving and climbing, before dropping scores of feet to engage each other in combat.

And below, the unmarked police car containing Dancer, Evans and King pulled to the kerb outside a pub where they'd decided to have a drink.

As the birds battled above them, the blood from their wounds rained out of the sky, followed by a loose drift of black and white feathers. But no bodies. As the birds died, they popped out of the air as if they had never been there.

The first spots of blood hit the car just as Dancer was closing the front passenger door. He looked in amazement as the scarlet drops marred the grubby white paintwork of the Vauxhall Cavalier.

Then more drops spattered on to the mackintosh he kept in the office for wet days, which he'd grabbed on the way out in case of more bad weather. It was a light-coloured Burberry and the blood hit, then spread across the cotton material, and Dancer was suddenly back in his nightmare, when the red rain had fallen out of a cloudless sky. He could barely suppress a scream.

'What is it?' said King, as spots of gore spattered on to her jacket. When she looked up, her face was splashed with red. 'What the *fuck* is it?'

'Back in the car,' shouted Evans, and they all dived into the Vauxhall, gaping in horror as the blood streaked the windscreen and coloured the pavement crimson.

As they watched, the first feathers began to float down to the ground. 'It's birds,' said Evans. 'It's fucking birds.'

'But what are they doing?' asked Jane King, shuddering as she wiped the blood off her face with a paper tissue.

'I don't know,' said Jack Dancer, and his own voice sounded strange in his ears. 'I just don't know.'

The blood fell on to the factory roof, too, and at first Trace thought it was the start of another storm, until drops started hitting the filthy windows and running down them in carmine streaks.

Even he was astounded and ran to the door, momentarily forgetting about Diana Collier. He stood in the doorway and looked up at the heavy scarlet rain that fell from a sky as blue as a cornflower.

The pair of crows watched too, and shivered in fear from the tops of their heads to the tips of their claws, because they knew what was happening above them, and that knowledge terrified them.

42

The battle for the skies raged for another half an hour, and news teams and a police helicopter rushed to report the phenomenon.

But just as the chopper arrived above Peckham, the last of the doves were driven off by the hawks, who were superior in power and numbers, and the hawks themselves regrouped and flew north at speed. And as the eggbeater rotors pulled the machine through the air to where the fight had taken place, the vermilion rain ceased.

Thousands of people had seen it, hundreds had been caught in it, and not one would forget the day the skies opened twice. Once with cold, hard, silver rain, and the second time with a warmer red shower that painted the city scarlet.

But, like the plagues that had once been visited upon Egypt, there was more to come.

Trace watched and marvelled at the whole thing, and had no more idea than anyone else about what had happened.

He heard the scream of sirens as police and other emergency services rushed around looking for injuries where there were none, and from the upstairs windows he saw ITN, BBC, CNN and Sky TV trucks tearing around looking for stories, and he smiled. The best story is here, he thought. Right under your noses and you can't see it.

Then he went back to the woman.

'It's time,' he said, and the earth beneath his feet began to shake.

43

The earthquake that devastated a small part of south London that hot and sticky summer evening registered a seven on the Richter scale. It was short, fierce and deadly. But it didn't stop Matthew Trace.

When the shock hit, he was knocked to the floor and he watched the examination table, with Diana Collier still tied to it, bunny hop across the room until it hit one of the walls and was still.

The small light that Trace always kept burning over the workbench winked out; but it was still light outside and, even though the filthy windows were still streaked with blood that had now turned brown in the air, it made little difference to his vision. He saw the solid concrete floor ripple like a wave on a lake, and tools started dropping on to the ground with a clatter.

Trace looked up and noticed that the solid roof of the factory, supported as it was by half a dozen steel RSJs, was moving too, and he suddenly wondered if it would come down and kill the pair of them.

But the roof held, and as the earth tremor abated after just a few seconds – (to Trace it seemed like hours – the building settled and was still again.

Christ, he thought as he pulled himself to his feet. This has been a hell of a day.

Outside, others had not been so lucky.

The quake hit just a few streets, and most of them were full of empty factories like the one Trace rented. But less than half a mile away, and still occupied, were two blocks of high-rise flats and a small terrace of two-storey houses that had not been demolished when the flats had been erected.

Most of the factories had been craftsmen-built in earlier times, and stayed standing, although a dozen or more sustained some damage. But the flats had been thrown up during the sixties, and were shoddy and should have been demolished years previously. Both blocks came down with a rumble like thunder, killing seventy-two people in all, and injuring another two hundred.

Half a dozen houses were completely destroyed too,

162

and in those another twelve people perished and twenty were injured.

Sewers, gas and water pipes fractured, phones were knocked out and the electricity supply to the area was cut off.

After the terrible noise of the quake and the buildings coming down in clouds of dust, there was perfect silence for a heartbeat, and then the screaming began.

Not that Trace could hear it inside the thick walls of the factory, and not that he would have cared if he had. But he did hear yet another chorus of sirens getting closer, as the full resources of London's public services were concentrated into one tiny area, and he realized that he would be unable to continue the unfinished business with the young pregnant woman he had kidnapped.

At least not for a while.

44

Trace walked towards the woman, over a floor now lumpy and uneven where the concrete had broken, and looked down at her.

Her hand was bruised and swollen, but the blood had clotted into a ragged scab at the joint of her finger.

'I wouldn't be at all surprised if we didn't get visitors soon,' said Trace as the sound of sirens got louder. 'So you're going to have to be hidden away. Don't worry, I won't forget about you.' And he pushed the wheeled table through to the other, larger portion of the factory where his vehicles were parked.

Some of the ceiling had come down in there and the cars and trucks were covered in dust, but a cursory examination showed that no serious damage had been done.

He pushed the gurney into the centre of the room, made sure all the windows were covered, that the door leading outside was locked, and after checking the webbing that fastened her to the bed, and that her gag was tight, he left, shutting and locking the door behind him.

The sirens were screaming by then, and he ran upstairs where he saw a fire appliance negotiating the street outside, bumping over the loose tarmac that the quake had dislodged. It stopped outside the factory gates, and half a dozen firemen got out. He saw them peering through the fence at the Cosworth that was parked up close to the front door.

'I thought so,' he said to himself and went down to meet them.

He walked to the gate, unlocked it and tried to swing it open, but the ground had shifted beneath it, and it took a concentrated effort from him and two of the firefighters to budge it. As they strained at it Trace saw that the gate itself and the ground around it was stained brown by the blood that had fallen from the skies that afternoon.

'Sorry, but it's buggered,' said one of the firemen when they finally managed to wrench it open to the sound of splintering wood. 'You'll have to get that fixed. I hope you're insured.'

'The landlord is,' said Trace in a friendly way. 'I'm

glad you came along, I'd never've been able to open it on my own.'

'Is everyone all right inside?' asked another fireman, whose white helmet marked him out as the captain of the crew.

'There's only me,' said Trace. 'What the hell happened? One minute I was doing some work, the next I was picking myself up off the floor after the place nearly came down around my ears.'

'Earthquake,' said the captain. 'Strictly local. No one's ever seen anything quite like it. Must be the weather.'

'Yeah, that's been weird too,' said Trace.

'Been a funny old day altogether, one way and another,' said the first fireman, and he looked at the ground. 'I see you got the blood too,' he said.

'Yeah. What was all that about?'

'God knows. Birds they say.'

'*Birds?*' said Trace.

'That's what they say. Fighting up in the sky. But do you know the strangest thing?'

Trace shook his head.

'All that blood, and loads of feathers. But not one body. Not one. There's something very strange going on in this part of the world.'

'You can say that again,' said Trace.

'Much damage?' asked the fire chief.

'Not a lot. These places were built to last. How big was the quake?'

'Big enough to bring down a couple of blocks of flats a dozen streets away. A lot of people hurt. Most of the rest of the lads are back there. They just sent us out to look for other damage, and get the area evacuated.

There's a lot of gas leaking out into the streets, and the sewers are gone. It's a health hazard.'

'There's not much life round here,' said Trace. 'Most of the places are closed down.'

'Yeah,' said the fireman. 'We'd better come in and take a look round. Do a damage report.'

Trace thought fast. There was no way they could come in. Not with Diana Collier inside, not to mention the bogus ambulance and police car. 'Can't it wait?' he said. 'I've an urgent delivery to make. Big job, important client, and I can't afford to make him wait. The roads are open, aren't they?'

'Just about. Go by the way of the Rye. You're going now?'

'That's right,' said Trace. 'Just as soon as I can make the gate secure.'

'What do you do in there, anyway?' asked the captain.

'Ironwork,' said Trace. It was a story he had invented months before, just in case the day arrived when he was questioned by some authority. That day *had* arrived. 'Fancy gates, that sort of thing.'

'Well, I'd get everything portable out as soon as possible. There might be aftershocks, and sometimes these places can be weakened without anyone noticing. We'll just take a quick shufti, then we'll leave you in peace. Unless we have to condemn the place,' he added darkly.

'No,' said Trace again. 'I'm going to move out permanently after all this. It's too dangerous. I'll lock up now and leave. And I won't be back except to collect my stuff. You'd be wasting your time.'

'It won't take long,' said the fireman. 'It's for your own good.'

'I know, but—' Trace was interrupted as the radio in the fire tender came to life and a voice, made harsh with static, filled the street.

'Shout, Guv,' said the driver, starting the engine.

'Damn,' said the captain wearily, then turned to Trace. 'For God's sake be careful. We'll be back if we can, but meanwhile my advice to you is to evacuate immediately.'

'I will,' said Trace with relief in his voice as the crew hauled themselves on to the fire engine, and it set off at speed, siren screaming.

Trace forced the gate closed and went back to the factory, on the way checking on the Cosworth, which looked fine, although the cobblestones of the courtyard had shifted considerably.

When he was safely inside, with the door fastened firmly behind him, Trace went back to Diana Collier. She was whimpering softly behind her gag at the pain from her hand, and her eyes widened with fear as he drew closer.

'Relax,' said Trace. 'No more today. There's too many nosy bastards around. You'll have to be my guest for a bit longer until they've gone, and we can have our fun in private.'

45

The worst of the quake missed the almost-deserted pub where Dancer and his colleagues were having a drink after the rain of blood, but they still felt its effect.

'Jesus. What now?' sighed the inspector as the room shuddered, bottles rattled, and half a dozen glasses smashed on the floor.

'This is unbelievable,' said Evans. Eventually the tremor stopped. 'I'm going to call in and find out what's happening.'

He rushed outside, and Dancer and King looked at each other. They were both pale from everything that had happened during the dreadful day.

Evans was back quickly. 'An earthquake,' he said. 'An earthquake in bleedin' Peckham. It's bad, but luckily local. Whittier and Broome are down.'

'What?' said Dancer.

'Whittier House and Broome House on Lawton Street. They came down. It's pandemonium down there. They're sending in crews to dig the survivors out now.'

As if to underline his words, the same sirens that Trace had heard wailed by.

'Christ,' said Dancer. 'What is going on?'

'Don't ask me, Boss,' said Evans, and for once the senior officer let it go.

'Want to take a look?' Evans went on.

'Might as well,' said Dancer. 'We might be able to do something to help.'

But there was nothing for them to do. Younger and

fitter men than the inspector and the sergeant were pulling bodies out of the rubble when they arrived, and it was better to leave it to the experts. Bodies were lined up on the grass and mud in front of what once had been the two blocks of flats. And although a main had ruptured, and a column of water fully thirty feet high was pouring down into the mud the storm had made of the ground, the air was still thick with a smoky powder from the collapse of the buildings, and a terrible crying was coming from some of the survivors still trapped. The news vans were back with a vengeance, and technicians and reporters were running around, hampering the rescuers and sneaking film of the victims. A couple of uniformed PCs were trying to contain the media people but with little success.

'This is awful,' said Jane King as she looked at some of the people who had been dragged clear, many minus arms or legs, most bleeding profusely, and as white as ghosts from the dust.

'We're doing no good here,' said Dancer. 'Let's go back to the station and see if they need us.'

Trace had no intention of leaving the factory for good, despite what he'd told the fireman, and despite the fact that there might be loose gas rolling down the road outside at that precise moment, ready to ignite if it found a spark.

All he did was to move the Cosworth round to the back of the factory, out of sight of the road, then go back in to Diana Collier.

'Strange things are happening,' he said. 'Very strange. It's almost as if someone doesn't want me to hurt you.

169

But I will. There's no electricity, but the nights are short these days and I don't think we'll miss it, do you?'

She made no kind of reply, just lay in her own filth and regarded him silently.

'You smell bad,' he said. 'But not as bad as you will. Anyway, I'm going to scope out the area, see if we're alone, and maybe see what's been happening all around the town. Don't go away, will you?'

Once again she made no kind of answer.

Trace left the building, climbed over the back fence and slid like a shadow down streets that were just beginning to be touched by twilight.

The area that the quake had hit was eerily quiet, not a soul stirred, and it looked as if the fireman's warning had been heeded by the rest of the population of that part of Peckham.

Trace walked along the buckled pavement avoiding the occasional downed lamppost and ducking through two more water mains that had exploded into fountains.

He realized he was thirsty, and when he saw a dark and dingy pub on one corner he tried the door. It was unlocked, and he stepped inside. The interior seemed deserted. He called out, 'Hello. Anyone there?'

There was no reply and he went behind the bar. The tills were open and empty. He tried one of the pumps, then remembered that the electricity was out, and opened the fridge. It was dark inside, but the bottles of imported beer were still cool. He opened one, finishing it almost in one draught.

'I hope you're going to pay for that,' said a voice, and despite himself, Trace jumped.

'Sorry. I didn't mean to frighten you,' and from the

gloom of a doorway at the far end of the bar a young man appeared. He was holding a glass full of dark liquid in one hand, a cigarette in the other, and appeared well on the road to being drunk.

'Bit quiet tonight,' he said with a slight slur in his voice. 'The passing trade seems to have vanished.'

'I was going to pay, as it happens,' said Trace. 'I did call out.'

'I heard you. I was frightened it was a gang of rapists.'

'Would that worry you?'

'Of course it would.'

'No, I'm not a rapist,' said Trace. 'I'm much worse than that.'

The young man giggled and came further into the bar.

'Is this your place?' asked Trace, helping himself to another beer, and placing a fiver on the bar.

'Sort of. My dad's the licensee. But he's away today. Typical. The biggest storm for a hundred years. Blood all over the windows, then a sodding earthquake, and the old man's gone to the races. Can't reach him on the phone. That's out. So I'm just waiting till he gets back, whenever the hell that's going to be.'

'You shouldn't have left the door open.'

'I didn't know I'd left it on the latch till you arrived. Some Old Bill came in a while ago, and told me they're evacuating. I said I'd go, but' – he lifted the glass he was holding – 'this seemed like the best option.'

'Dangerous, though,' said Trace. 'Especially if you're frightened.'

'But you look all right.' The young man came even closer. 'Very all right, I'd say.'

Trace could smell the young man's odour, and the

liquor and tobacco on his breath, and it almost made him retch.

'Want another beer?' the boy asked. 'On the house. Then maybe I could lock up and we could go into the back.'

'I'm not like that,' said Trace, barely containing his anger.

'Course you are. All men are, when there's no one around. They'll fuck anything that's wet and warm.'

'What about your father?'

'He'll be hours yet. I've got a little battery TV in the kitchen. Apparently the traffic's jammed up for miles around. He'll just stop and go into another pub.'

'He'll be worried.'

'What, him? If the place had come down around my ears and crushed me to death, the first thing he'd think about was the insurance. So are you coming, or what?' And he licked his lips.

'You won't like it if I do,' said Trace.

'I'm sure I will.'

'Because I'll hurt you.'

'I don't mind being hurt.'

'You'll mind this.'

'Let's wait and see.'

'On your own head be it.'

'Suits me.'

Trace took a third beer as the young man locked the front door of the pub. Some of the last of the sun was shining through the window, and the boy looked frail and girlish in its light. Trace smiled to himself as he sipped at the beer, before the boy led him towards the door he'd come through, and into the back of the pub.

46

The room behind the bar was a clutter of boxes and old furniture, with the only new item being a big-screen TV that looked balefully from the corner with its single grey, dead eye.

'My room's through here,' said the boy. 'Come on.'

His room was a muddle too, with piles of clothes, magazines, CDs and tapes lying everywhere.

The bed was a full double, and he swept the junk that was on top of it on to the floor, then started to undress.

Trace watched him as he began to unbutton the loose, thin, floral shirt he was wearing.

'Come on,' the boy said. 'What are you waiting for?'

He moved closer until they were about two feet apart. 'You remember when I said I was worse than a gang of rapists?' said Trace.

The young man nodded and smiled uncertainly.

'I was telling the truth,' and Trace swung a loping left to the boy's jaw, knocking him on to the greasy carpet.

As he lay there, Trace kicked him in the face. The boy lay still, Trace took him by the arm and dragged him up on to the bed.

He went back into the store-cum-sitting room and found a length of twine with which he tied the boy's hands and feet together.

Then he went looking for the kitchen.

He found the cutlery drawer and a sharp paring knife, and went back to the boy's room where he was just coming round.

He opened his mouth to scream when he saw Trace, but the Torturer was too fast for him and slapped it shut. 'Don't make a sound,' he said, and showed the boy the weapon.

He sat on the edge of the bed and doodled a pattern on the boy's bare stomach, which showed through the open front of his shirt, with the point of the implement. 'What's your name?' he asked.

'Kevin,' the boy managed to stutter. 'Don't kill me.'

Trace smiled and ran the knife down between the boy's legs.

'I've got one like you at home,' he said. 'At least almost like you. So I need to get a little practice in.'

The boy threw himself across the bed in a mad scramble to escape, but Trace simply reached over, grabbed him by the hair and tugged him back.

'I warned you, you'd be sorry,' he said.

He bent close so that he could smell the boy's odour again, but now it was subtly charged with another smell. A smell that Trace knew well. The smell of fear. It made him feel almost lightheaded.

'Don't do that again,' he said. 'Or I may lose my temper.' And he slashed the knife viciously across the boy's chest, opening a large slice in his smooth skin that immediately began to pour blood.

The boy, ashen with fear, made one more desperate bid for freedom, but he was too slow, and Trace caught him easily. He began to cut the boy's body again, lifting up huge flaps of skin. Blood sprayed in all directions, spattering across the bed, up the walls and all over Trace's own clothes.

He stabbed at the boy's face with the point of the

blade, plunging the steel deep into his neck and mouth, snapping off teeth as it went. Then he moved up the boy's face, slicing open his nose and smashing the knife down into his brain.

The boy didn't take long to die, voiding his bladder and bowels, and hammering his heels on the bed as he did so.

Trace ignored the stench and began to hack through his neck. This had been the most wonderful killing of his life, and he needed a souvenir.

When the boy's head was lying on the gore-drenched pillow, Trace wiped himself on the sheet and went looking for a suitable container for it. He found a bag from Tower Records under the bed and slid the head into it, bunching up the top and tying it securely with twine.

Then he searched the place until he found an old mackintosh to put over his sodden clothes.

On the way out he put another five pound note next to the first one.

He was back in the factory with his prize in a few minutes, not seeing a soul as he went through empty streets. It was the time of midsummer when it hardly seems to get dark at all, the short night retaining the light from the day, and holding it in its grasp until the early dawn. Trace needed no street lamps to guide his way back.

47

Trace tossed the bagged head over the fence at the back of the factory. It landed with a dull thud and he followed it, retrieved the parcel and went inside.

Before he went to see Diana Collier, he found some stubs of candles which he lit, then took the head out of the Tower Records bag that was now awash at the bottom with blood and brain fluid. He smoothed down the bedraggled dark hair, and set the head on a workbench which had tilted in the earthquake, but was still standing bolted to the wall. He regarded it with satisfaction, took off the mackintosh he was wearing, dropped it carelessly on the floor, and went into the back.

The woman was exactly where he'd left her, still lying on her back on the examination table, securely bound and looking up into the darkness of the sealed room.

As Trace entered, allowing a little dim light to filter in from the other room, she turned her eyes in his direction. They were dull and lifeless now, as if she had spent the time she'd been alone contemplating her fate, and realizing that the forecast was nothing but bad.

If she noticed his bloodstained hands and clothes, she made no sign.

'I've been practising,' said Trace. 'Now we can go for the main event. And I've got someone I'd like you to meet.' He wheeled the table back the way he'd come.

Diana Collier saw the head staring sightlessly at her from its place of honour on the tilted workbench. She screamed into her gag. The head reclined somewhat drunkenly, resembling the Gorgon of legend as the hair on the skull dried into snake-like fronds, and the candle-light cast strange shadows over its waxy skin.

'This is my friend Kevin. Kevin, meet Diana. Diana, meet Kevin.' But neither said a word.

Trace stood and looked down at Diana Collier and said, 'Now we begin.'

He started by putting out her eyes so that she would not see what was happening. He popped each eyeball with the point of a long scalpel, then cauterized the wounds with an electronic gas cigarette lighter turned up full so that the pressurized blue flame was almost an inch long. She writhed in her bonds as he burnt out her eyes and almost bit through the tape that covered her mouth, so that he had to put on another layer of gaffer.

She began to miscarry after that. The pain was too much for her body. Something primeval inside her told her that she was soon to die, and she wanted to give her child one chance to live. She started to contract, and Trace watched as the baby's head began to show. It was covered in blood and placenta.

But it was too early, far too early, for the baby to live without an incubator and expert attention.

Trace looked at it coldly as it tried to catch a breath, but failed.

'Don't worry,' he said to Diana Collier's still form. 'You'll soon get your figure back.' And he plunged the length of the scalpel blade into her distended belly close to her navel, and was rewarded with a gush of blood that splattered him from head to toe in its warmth.

She died there, on the table, and Trace tore the baby's body from her and threw it into the corner.

He was acting as if possessed, and in his blood frenzy he did not hear the enormous clap of thunder that burst out of the clear sky, scaring the two crows that were still perched outside watching, and finally sending them winging back across London to their master.

48

Trace stepped away from Diana Collier's body and looked at the results of his labours with satisfaction. He wiped the blood from his face, then turned to the head that stood on the bench. 'Too quick, Kevin. Too bloody quick,' he said.

'Not at all,' said a deep rasping voice from the shadows in the corner of the room. 'Not at all.'

Trace spun round, his hand reaching for any weapon on the bench. He cursed himself for not having his gun, cocked and loaded and close by.

'It wouldn't do any good if you did have it,' said the voice, and a dapper figure appeared from where it had watched Trace kill Diana Collier and the foetus. 'Guns can't hurt me.'

'How did you know . . .?' said Trace, as it seemed the figure had read his mind.

'I know everything. The where, why and who.'

Trace looked in amazement as the figure got closer. The man was about five foot six, dressed in a neat pinstriped suit with a white shirt and bow tie. His minuscule feet were shod in shiny black shoes, and in one tiny hand he carried a leather briefcase with brass locks and hinges. 'Everything,' he repeated, and Trace could hardly believe that such a massive voice could come from such a tiny figure.

Although the man's appearance was unexceptional, except for his size, something about him emanated such an aura of evil that Trace backed up as far as he could, until he felt the weight of the factory wall behind him. 'Who are you?'

'A good question,' said the man. 'But life's too short to explain. At least a human life is too short. We'd be here for years.'

'How did you get in?'

'Just let's say I'm here and leave it at that.'

Trace's eyes looked through the gathering dark at the detritus of his day's work.

'Don't worry,' said the man. 'I'm not here to bring you to justice or anything as mundane as that. I'm here to reimburse you.'

'What?'

'You agreed to do a job for a fee. You were paid ten per cent in advance. This is the balance.' And he threw the case on to the bench, next to the severed head. 'You'll need some light to count it.' And he spat a gob of flame that ignited the boy's hair like a torch. 'Go on,' said the man. 'It won't bite you.'

Trace could hardly believe his eyes at what he had seen. He looked from the man to the burning head in amazement, then pulled himself together and said, 'But I didn't get the information. Collier died.'

'You did the job that needed doing. You killed the child.' And the figure spat another gob of flame at the baby's body, so that too burst into flames, emitting a greasy, foul-smelling smoke. 'Go on, count the money,' the man roared. And for a second Trace thought that the figure was going to change into something else, something that existed at the edge of his consciousness, like a memory he had never seen, but he blinked and it was gone. Trace did as the figure ordered and reached for the case and popped the locks.

By the light from the burning head, Trace saw that the briefcase was stuffed with money. Quickly he riffled through the stacks of fifty pound notes until he'd counted exactly the amount he was owed.

'All present and correct?' asked the figure.

Trace nodded.

'Never let it be said that I renege on a deal,' said the figure. 'Now, I warn you, what you have done today has marked you for ever as an outcast in this world and the next. Powerful forces tried to stop you fulfilling the commission, but they were thwarted.' The man smiled at the word, and Trace saw that his teeth were long and white. 'You see, *I* prevailed. However, those same forces and their allies will not cease until you are destroyed. I'll help you when I can, although even I cannot promise you that I will always succeed. But you knew long ago that you chose a path that would one day end at the doors of hell. So be warned. All you need to do to summon me is snap your fingers. I'm going now. We may meet again, we may not. I hope for your sake it is the latter.'

'But who are you?' repeated Trace, his mind full of unanswered questions.

'You don't want to know, believe me.'

'I do.'

'Then I'll show you. But on your own head be it.'

And as the figure backed away from Trace, its form began to change. It grew and grew until it stood ten feet tall and strangely beautiful. The neat suit and tie turned into black scales above the waist, and luxurious dark fur beneath, covering its long muscular legs down to the black cloven hooves that metamorphosed out of the neat black shoes. Its shoulders and chest broadened, arms swelling with muscle. Its head was black too. Bald, except for a covering of smaller scales, and its eyes gleamed bright and yellow. The pure white teeth length-ened, and seemed to become even whiter in comparison with the black skin that stretched across its high cheek-bones. And out of its back grew a pair of wings, black and delicate as gossamer, and webbed with veins.

'Satisfied?' it roared, and stepped further back into the darkness at the corners of the room, which deepened as the fires from the human flesh began to flicker and die. And the last thing that Trace heard was the clatter of its hooves as the Great Beast vanished into the shadows.

Trace followed, but it was gone. Shit, he thought. Was I dreaming? But the head of the boy and the body of the dead child were still smoking, and he knew that he was not.

He stood for a moment, then, shaking, he stumbled to the bench, unlocked the drawer, took out the Beretta and reassembled it. He left the silencer where it was and took the gun upstairs. He washed the blood off himself and changed his clothes, tucked the gun into his belt and left the factory and its grisly contents for the last time.

49

The two crows arrived back at Mariella Newman's house just as Trace was counting the money, and they cawed their news softly into the Crow Man's ears. But he had heard the single clap of thunder and already knew what it meant. He listened, nevertheless, and his face darkened.

When his two emissaries had finished their report, he smoothed their ruffled feathers with his fingers and cooed back to them that they were brave and loyal fellows, and that he would not forget them. Then he stepped over the stinking bodies of the slaughtered crows, which now wriggled with maggots, and went downstairs to where their murderer was sitting, nursing the brandy bottle and looking through the window at nothing but her memories.

'It is finished,' he announced as he stepped through the door.

'What is finished?' she asked.

'The job that Trace was destined to do.'

Her eyes, as dark and cold as underground pools, swept round to look at him. 'And is he mine now?'

'Perhaps. Perhaps not.'

'What do you mean?'

The Crow Man knelt on the floor before her and said, 'Listen, mistress, and listen well.' He gripped her hand as he spoke. It was the first time he had ever touched her, and she found that his fingers were freezing. When the cuff of his jacket pulled up, she saw that instead of hairs on the back of his arm there were tiny black feathers, and she shivered.

'Have you not seen the way the world is going? You should be aware of that better than anyone, after what has happened to you. Have you not seen the atrocities and cruelty that occur? The way it is run by criminals. Your world is going through its menopause. It was a young world when it began, and it will be an old world when it finishes. And then beware, because chaos will reign, as you have never seen it before.'

He paused for her reaction, but there was none.

'The gate to hell has always existed. And across the ages many mortals have discovered its whereabouts, and used it to their own ends. Good men and evil men have passed through it. But nothing but evil has ever emerged. The good men have been corrupted because the guardians of the door can see into men's hearts, and know what they really desire, and can supply it. The list is long and heartbreaking: Alexander, Caesar, Atilla, Bonaparte, Rasputin, Hitler, Kennedy. All these men and dozens more discovered the door to hell, and all were defiled, no matter how noble their original intentions.'

'And where is this gate?'

'It comes and goes from place to place. Europe, Asia, the Americas. And sometimes it is nowhere.'

'Where is it *now*, you fool?'

'In this city. In a dirty little place underneath the building where Trace operates.'

'And what was this special job?'

'There is good as well as evil at work here. If that were not so, this world would have been destroyed long ago. The powers of good have long wished to close the gate, and finally they decided to send one of their own to do it. A certain couple in the city were chosen. They were picked to produce the child who would grow into the man who could do the deed. He was to be born in two months' time. But the devil himself discovered the plan. Now, although he exists in men's hearts and minds, he's unable to do the deed himself. Only a mortal could do it. That was Trace's job. To prevent the birth of the one person who could close the gate for good, by aborting the baby that was growing inside Diana Collier. And today he succeeded.'

'The child *died*?'

'Yes. And the mother. And another man.'

Guilt rushed through Mariella Newman's veins again. She realized that she had been a fool.

The Crow Man saw her distress and said, 'Do not blame yourself, mistress. It was not your fault.'

'So that is why we could not deal with Trace before?' she said.

'Correct. We are no match for Satan himself.'

'Is there no end to it?'

'No. The seeds of destruction were sown at the birth of the world. Today they came to fruit. There will be much celebration at the devil's table tonight.'

'What can we do?'

'I don't know, mistress.'

'There must be something.'

'I'm sorry. I fear it is too late.'

50

As Trace was driving away from Peckham, and Mariella Newman and the Crow Man were deep in conversation in Kensington, Dancer, Evans and King were sitting in Dancer's office discussing the bizarre events of the day, when the phone rang.

It was the uniformed sergeant in charge of the communication centre downstairs. 'We've got a bad one, sir,' he said.

'What kind of bad one?'

'A dead man. Mutilated.'

'Where?'

'A pub called the Hawk and Dove. On Upton Street, right in the quake zone.'

'I know it. Why me? There's a lot of bodies down there. I've seen some of them.'

'This one's different. A murder.'

'Are you sure?'

'Sure as I can be. Whoever did it cut off his head and took it with him.'

'What?'

'Yeah, I thought it would be right up your street.'

'Who reported it?'

'The lad's father. The landlord. Chap name of Kenny Rowlands.'

'Christ, I know him, and his boy. Kevin, isn't it?'

'Correct. There's uniforms down there now. He's in a shocking state by all accounts.'

'We're on our way.'

Evans spun the car through the still gridlocked streets using his siren and flashing headlights to cut a swathe through the traffic, and barely five minutes after Dancer had received the call they tumbled out of the car. The whole pub was brightly lit by portable arc lights, and police cars and ambulances were parked topsy turvy outside.

The first constable they met was busy taping the area off. Dancer flashed his ID and said, 'What's it like inside?'

The young policeman's face was very pale in the strong white light. 'Shocking,' he said.

'Show me,' said Dancer.

The PC took them into the bar, where Kenny Rowlands was sitting on one of the bench seats holding a full glass of whisky unsteadily in both trembling hands, slops dripping down on to his trouser legs. Next to him was sitting a uniformed policewoman, and a paramedic was standing close by.

'Mr Rowlands,' said Dancer.

'I know you, don't I?' said the man.

'I've drunk here. Jack Dancer. Inspector. Peckham CID. What happened?'

'Well, I'm not sure . . . I was off to the races. Kev was in charge . . .' He broke off. 'But then that storm happened . . . and some weird thing with blood. And an earthquake. I couldn't believe it. I was stuck on the road. Couldn't get through on the car phone. I got back, the place was wide open, and . . .'

He couldn't continue, just spilled more of his drink down his trousers and started to cry.

'Look after him, love,' said Dancer to the police-woman, and the uniformed constable showed them through to the back room.

SOCO, fingerprints and forensics were everywhere, and the PC pointed Dancer and Co. in the direction of the bedroom.

Dancer walked across the threshold of Kevin Rowlands' bedroom, Evans close behind him, King bringing up the rear. He stopped dead, the sergeant barely managed not to step on his heels. The room appeared to have been painted red by an amateur decorator. There was blood everywhere; on the walls, on the carpet, and especially on the bed, where it had soaked through the covers and pooled on top like unpleasant soup. And lying in the midst of the gore was the headless corpse of the boy.

'Jesus Christ,' said Dancer.

Evans just shook his head. He and his superior had seen so many terrible sights recently that he was almost immune to them. Jane King paled and turned away, her hand flying to her mouth to suppress a gag.

The medical examiner had finished his preliminary examination and was pulling the rubber gloves from his hands when he saw Dancer's squad's entrance. 'Hello, Jack,' he said. 'Welcome to the house of fun.'

Dancer shook his head, and asked, although it was hardly necessary, 'Cause of death?'

'Let's rule out natural causes, shall we?' said the ME. 'Multiple stab wounds should do it. Unless he shot him in the head first with a small calibre bullet that lodged in the skull.'

'We've got the knife, Guv,' said a forensic man, and held up a plastic bag. 'Covered in blood,' he added.

'I can see that,' snapped Dancer.

The forensic man pulled a face.

Dancer went closer to the bed and looked down at the body. 'But why take the poor sod's head?' he said to no one in particular.

'Some people just can't bear to go home without a souvenir,' said the ME. 'Unless, of course, he did shoot him, and wanted the bullet back, but I very much doubt it. Looks like an ordinary kitchen knife to me. Probably picked it up here. No, I reckon this was an opportunist killing. Anyway, I'd better get back and do my report, then you can get this poor bugger somewhere decent. But I reckon whatever happens it's going to be a closed-casket funeral.' And with that he left.

The trio of detectives stood for a while around the bed as the scene of crime officers got on with their grisly task, and then they went back into the bar.

'Somebody had a drink, Guv,' said one of the fingerprint officers, pointing at the two bottles of Sol that stood alone on the back of the bar. 'And whoever it was left ten quid.' The notes that Trace had put down were still where he'd left them, one clean and one stained with blood.

'How very honest of him,' said Dancer. 'And talking of drinks, I could use one myself,' he added.

Rowlands, who was still sitting with the WPC, said, 'Help yourself.'

'And there's another bottle and a glass in the bed-room,' said the FO.

'You finished here?' Dancer asked him.

'As we'll ever be. SOCO's got to bag the bottles and the cash. Otherwise we've done.'

Dancer picked up three clean glasses and a bottle of Calvados from the bar and poured three large drinks. 'I know we're on duty,' he said as he pushed one each in front of Evans and King. 'But I think we need these.'

The two junior officers gratefully picked up their drinks and all three dispatched them with a swallow.

'Right,' said Dancer. 'Let's get started.'

51

Dancer left the other officers and went over to Kenny Rowlands. 'Sorry,' he said. 'But there's a couple of things I have to know.'

Rowlands looked up. 'Go on then.'

'What time did you get back here?'

'Ten. Just after.'

'And the front door was locked?'

'No.'

'What did you do?'

'I thought he'd be inside waiting. It was dark in the bar. All the electrics were off. I called out Kev's name, and Jim and Dave – that's the two staff who were here when I left – but I got no answer, so I went through to the back room, then into his bedroom.' He stopped.

'It must've been awful,' said Dancer.

Rowlands looked up at him again, and his eyes were a thousand years old. 'It was pitch in there,' he said. 'But it stank. I couldn't place the smell. I used my lighter. I couldn't believe my eyes,' and he started to sob.

'He was gay, wasn't he?' said Dancer.

'Yeah,' replied Rowlands. 'My boy. A fuckin' poof.'

'Do you think it was someone he knew?'

'I don't know, honest.'

'I'm sorry, Mr Rowlands,' said Dancer. 'I realize how upsetting this must be for you. But I must have the addresses of your two staff. I need to interview them right away. Then I'll leave you alone.'

'In the book behind the bar. Hanging on the nail there.'

Jane King reached for the notebook that was looped by a piece of string from a crooked nail banged into the plaster.

'Back page,' said Rowlands. 'Jim Flynn and Dave Morgan.'

King quickly copied down the two men's names, addresses and telephone numbers, then put the book back where she'd found it.

'Thank you, Mr Rowlands,' said Dancer. 'Is there anywhere you'd like to go? I can get you a car.'

'I live here,' said Rowlands.

'Not tonight, I don't think,' said Dancer compassionately. 'Isn't there anywhere else?'

'My sister in Lewisham.'

'If you tell the WPC the number, she'll get it organized. I take it your sister doesn't know.'

Rowlands shook his head.

'The PC will see to everything,' said Dancer. 'Won't you?'

The young policewoman nodded. 'Leave it with me, sir.'

'And I'll talk to you again soon,' Dancer said to Rowlands. 'When you're more up to it.'

'That'll be never,' said Rowlands. 'Listen, Mr Dancer. Kevin wasn't everything I wanted him to be, you know that. But try and catch whoever did it. He didn't deserve what happened to him. No one does.'

Dancer nodded, then went back to his squad. 'Come on then,' he said. 'We've got people to see.'

The rest of the night was spent interviewing the two male bar staff, who told the officers that as soon as the earthquake had subsided, at about seven thirty, Kevin Rowlands had shooed out the customers and let the bar staff go. They'd told him that he should leave too, but he'd refused. They then alibied each other by heading down to Peckham Rye and spending the rest of the evening drinking together. This was later confirmed by at least three witnesses.

Then a young police officer came forward with the information that he'd found Kevin Rowlands alone in the bar some time after eight, tried to convince him to leave, and had also been rebuffed. After he'd refused to join the boy in a drink, he had left and headed towards the demolished blocks of flats.

Then they checked with SOCO, fingerprints and forensics. By then the paring knife had been identified as the murder weapon, unless some fatal injury had been inflicted on the head before it was hacked off, and they had found that there were identifiable fingerprints on the three bottles. There was a partial palm print on the knife and one full hand print, in blood, on the bedroom door, plus more bloody finger marks on the second banknote found by the till. The fingerprint officer in charge was waiting for information from the computer. Forensics informed them that the killer must have been heavily bloodstained, and from portions of bloody footprints they had found, they surmised that he had left the pub and headed further into the earthquake zone.

That was it. By 1 a.m. that was the full extent of their knowledge.

'If he's got a record, we've got him,' said Evans.

'And if he hasn't?' Dancer said.

'We'll have to do door to door.'

'There's no one there,' said King. 'Our boys and the firemen got nearly everyone out.'

'He was still in there after eight-fifteen,' said Dancer. 'Jane, get on to the ambulance and fire stations. Let's find out who *was* in there. There must've been some others who insisted on sticking it out.'

And there were a few. Including, as one fire chief told them, the young man who ran the ironworks in the old factory in Porterdown Road.

By then it was 2.15 a.m., and the bad news came through that the fingerprints found at the crime scene could not be matched by the police computer. On that happy note the three detectives went home for some well-earned rest, agreeing to meet the following day in the earthquake zone.

*

It took the police until mid morning to get as far as the old factory. Painstakingly, they went from house to house trying to find if anyone had seen anything unusual, as if nothing unusual had happened all day.

But from the few remaining residents, they got no fresh information. Anyone who'd managed to survive had spent the evening with their heads well down.

Dancer and King got to the factory at 11 a.m. on that steamy morning, and found the broken gates pushed shut, with a chain looped through the stanchions on the street side, and a heavy-duty padlock fastening them.

'Looks like he went in the end,' said King, as Evans turned the corner after yet another fruitless interview.

'Looks like it,' replied Dancer, and he raised his head as if sniffing the air. 'But there's something strange about this place.'

'What?'

'A smell. I don't know.'

Jane King sniffed and shook her head. 'I can't smell it.'

Dancer looked at the gate which leaned drunkenly towards him. Evans joined them. 'What's up?'

'Dunno. Jane, do you reckon you could get through there?'

'I suppose so. But we don't have a warrant.'

'Gas leak,' said Dancer. 'I told you I smelled something.'

'OK,' said King. 'I'm glad I've got trousers on.' She hoisted herself up, and dropped down on the other side of the gates.

'Anything?' shouted Dancer.

'The door to the main block's ajar,' said King. 'And

now I know what you mean by the smell. I'll just go and have a look.'

'OK. But be careful.' And he and Evans listened as the heels of her shoes tap tap tapped across the cobblestones.

They heard her push the squeaky door open, and call out. 'Police. Anybody there?'

It was all quiet for a moment, then they heard her footsteps again, faster this time, and she was making a strange sound.

'What?' called Dancer.

'Get this fucking gate open,' Jane King screamed with more than a hint of hysteria in her voice. 'For pity's sake get it open and let me out of here.'

52

They opened the gate by the simple expedient of driving their car straight through it. It took Evans less than twenty seconds to do the deed, and they found Jane King kneeling on the cobbles, hugging herself tightly. Dancer ran to her, but she shook him off and pointed towards the dark hulk of the factory building. 'It's a baby,' was all she managed to say.

Dancer and Evans rushed inside, and by the dim light from the windows witnessed for themselves the horror she'd seen.

The interior of the factory stank with the odour of burned flesh, and the sweeter smell of bodies beginning to putrefy in the heat. It buzzed with the sound of the flies that had begun to feast on the corruption Trace had left behind.

Dancer walked over to the barely recognizable form of the baby, then looked at Diana Collier's body, and finally the misshapen lump of blackened bone that stood on the bench, which, as he feared, was Kevin Rowlands' head.

'I want this place cordoned off,' he said to Evans. 'I want SOCO, forensics and fingerprints down here pronto, and get a doctor for Jane.'

'I'm all right, sir,' said Jane King from the doorway. 'It was just a bit of a shock, that's all.'

'No you're not,' said Dancer.

'I am. I have to be. This is our man, isn't it?'

Dancer nodded.

'Then I'm going to be all right. At least until we catch the bastard. Then I can have my nervous breakdown in peace.'

Dancer looked at her hard and long. 'If you say so,' he said. 'Evans. Get on the radio.'

Within an hour, the old factory resembled an ants nest of activity. The outside was taped off, and technicians were everywhere hunting for evidence.

Outside the gates, a mobile HQ had been set up amidst the clutter of official cars, and Dancer and his squad, now strengthened by another half a dozen detectives were *in situ*.

'Looks like we missed him by half a day,' said Dancer. 'And I reckon he won't be back.'

'He won't when he spots what's going on,' said a DS named Reese.

'I don't think he would anyway,' said Dancer. 'It has an abandoned feel. And he's always moved the bodies before. This time he just left them. Anyway, I couldn't just order an obbo. Firstly I had to give the remains of those poor bastards inside some dignity. And also he might've noticed the state of his front gate.'

'Made a bit of a mess of the old Cavalier, Guv,' interjected a wag from the back of the room. 'Looks like the Council Tax'll have to be increased next year.'

'OK,' said Dancer through the ensuing laughter. 'You've had your fun. Now it's time to get down to business. We're on the site where our man, the so called Torturer, operated. Arrogant bastard. You can see the nick from the top floor. Up to now he's been cool. Done the jobs, then disposed of the bodies, neat as you like. But something happened yesterday, and he went mental with that kid in the boozer. And I want to know what it was.'

'A lot of things happened yesterday,' said Evans. 'I'm not surprised he went mental.'

He was interrupted by a rap on the plywood door of the office, and King opened it. Outside was the chief forensic officer. 'A word,' he said to Dancer, and the DCI stepped outside and closed the door behind him.

'God alone knows what's been going on inside that place,' said the CFO. 'We've found traces of at least a dozen different blood samples. We're going to have to DNA them to find out how many individuals were involved, and test them against the tissues of the murder victims you've been investigating. There's fingerprints galore too, and one set match the ones we got in the pub yesterday. Not that that shows much deductive genius with that poor bloke's head on display.'

'Any ID on the other woman yet?'

'No. But there was a report from Putney yesterday of a seven-months pregnant woman going missing. It's a strange case. The husband ran out of his place of business like he had the hounds of hell after him, and later he ended up getting killed by a falling billboard in the storm.'

'Name?'

'Stephen Collier.'

'I'll get it checked out. Anything else?'

'Not so far. But it's early days yet. Want to come and have a look round?'

'I'll be with you in a minute. I've just got to get this lot in here busy, then I'll come inside.'

Dancer allotted tasks to the new members of his squad, which mainly consisted of renewed house-to-house calls that he knew would be frustrated by the lack of residents in the area, although people were gradually starting to creep back to their homes. Dancer, Evans and King went back into the factory. Dancer had told Jane King that she could pass if she wished, but she agreed to return.

The electrical power had finally been restored and the few lights inside had been augmented by a battery of arc lights, under which the technicians toiled in the rising heat.

The two bodies and the head had been put into zip-up body bags in readiness for transportation to the mortuary for post mortems, and the fly population had thankfully decreased, but the place still stank of death and Jane King shivered when she entered, despite the high temperature.

'It's bloody hot in here,' she said.

'Are you going to be all right?' asked Dancer, again.

'I'm not made of porcelain,' she said, almost snapping. 'I'm a copper. And a bloody good one. It was just a bit of a shock, that's all.'

'OK, Jane,' said the DCI. 'I won't ask again.'

'Sorry, Guv. Bad day.'

'I understand.' Dancer squeezed her arm reassuringly.

They surveyed the downstairs area, and one of the technicians showed them what they had found so far: Trace's collection of fake IDs, the stolen ambulance and the vehicles tricked up to look like public service vehicles, a spent 9mm cartridge case, a box of bullets for the Beretta, and the collection of portable phones. 'This place is a treasure trove,' said the man. 'We'll be here for a week, I bet.'

'You'll see this stuff gets back to the nick?' said Dancer.

'Leave it to me. And be careful, you lot. This bloke's loaded for bear.'

'We will.'

Then the trio went upstairs to where Trace had occasionally slept and eaten his frugal meals.

'So this is his lair,' said Jane King.

'Or one of them,' said Dancer.

'But where the hell is he?' asked Evans.

53

Right then, Trace was sitting in his flat in Streatham trying to remember exactly what had happened the previous day.

He knew that something had possessed him. Something out of the normal run of events, even for him, and he wasn't pleased.

How could I have done that? he asked himself. Lost it completely. Anyone could have walked into that pub, or seen me on the way back to the factory.

He felt that maybe he'd dreamed it all, but the crusted blood under his fingernails when he'd got to the flat, and the vivid memories of what he'd done to the woman and the baby convinced him otherwise.

He also knew, after the fire crew's visit to the factory, that the Peckham site was blown, and that all his carefully gathered identification and expensively acquired vehicles were gone.

And, despite himself, he remembered the Great Beast that had visited him and warned him of his possible fate, and he touched the gun that he'd carried ever since for reassurance.

He could almost see in his mind's eye the activity around the old factory, and wondered how many clues he'd left to his identity there.

Should he run, or should he dig in and lie low? Those were the questions that ran through his mind as he sat and watched the sun move across the heavens, casting its light on both the good and the evil that men did on earth, without prejudice.

Mariella Newman watched the same sun. As it moved far enough around the sky to cast its rays through the window of her first-floor room, she began to brew her spell. She had been waiting patiently, with a book in her hand. She'd removed the book, wrapped in white muslin, from its hiding place in a trunk she had brought with her from Mexico.

She was dressed all in white, and had showered, washed her hair and combed it out straight, so that it hung almost to her waist.

She had ripped up the carpet and washed the floorboards beneath it thoroughly that morning.

She placed the book carefully in the middle of the floor and drew a pentagram with black chalk.

At each point of the star she wrote out the words in the language she hardly understood, exactly as they were written on the parchment pages.

Then she placed five black candles in five pewter candlesticks, one at each point.

Satisfied, she stood back and surveyed her handiwork before carefully replacing the book in its covering and returning it to its hiding place.

Then she poured herself a large brandy, sat on the sofa with her back to the window, so that the last of the sun bathed her in its radiance, and waited for midnight.

On the first stroke from the grandfather clock in the corner, which she had set precisely to the second, she lit the candles, and began to intone the chant she had learned off by heart.

As she spoke, the air above the pentagram shimmered like air over an empty frying pan on high heat, and the room filled with the smell of burning sulphur. Mariella's eyes watered and tears ran down her cheeks. But she kept speaking.

Then on the last word of the mantra, with a noise like a jet breaking the sound barrier, a dark figure materialized inside the protection of the pentangle.

Mariella had never seen anything like it, and involuntarily urinated, the hot liquid running down her legs and dripping on to the floor.

Whatever place the figure had originated in must have been as twisted and ugly as the figure itself.

He, because it undoubtedly was a he, stood no more than four feet tall, but was almost as broad.

Its head was tiny, and attached straight to its shoulders without any neck, so that to turn its gaze it had to turn its whole upper body.

The skull was misshapen and lumpy, and the top of it was covered with tufts of dirty black hair that stuck out in all directions. Its eyes were tiny, black and malevolent, and peered out from under a forehead that sloped back sharply to the hairline. And what appeared to be a pair of aborted horns protruded from each side. The nose reminded Mariella of a pig's snout, it dripped with mucus, and its mouth was lipless and jagged, the teeth yellow and sharp. The tongue, which lapped out every few seconds, was long, forked at the end, and obscenely red in colour.

It had no ears, just a hole at either side of its head, where ears would normally have been, surrounded by ugly scar tissue.

Its torso was thick and muscular, also covered with a growth of coarse hair, and had three nipples. Long arms ropey with muscle scraped the ground, and the six fingers on each hand were deformed with arthritic-looking knuckles.

Its legs were short and thick and also corded with muscle. But the most prominent feature of the naked being that stood before her, and the one thing that displayed its gender with absolute certainty, was the huge penis that jutted erect from the thatch of even darker hair between its legs.

It was fully twelve inches long and as thick as a baby tree. The scrotum that hung below was huge too, swollen with semen which ejaculated every few seconds and sizzled on the floor. Just looking at it, Mariella knew that if the liquid was to squirt into her body it would burn like boiling wax. But despite the horrific aspect of the monstrous being, she felt another wetness flood her vagina as she looked at its giant appendage. A wetness that she had not felt since before her husband had died, and she hated herself for the desire that flooded her body.

The beast turned itself towards her, leered and licked its lips again, before, in a voice that sounded as if it came from inside a rusty bucket, said, 'Want some, lady?' and began to masturbate its huge erection.

'Come on. Come inside and I'll give you a treat.'

Despite the lubrication which joined the urine as it ran down her legs, and the almost light-headed feeling to just say yes, break inside the pentagram and submit to the demon's attentions, Mariella said, 'No.'

'Then what the hell *do* you want?' The beast let out a

high-pitched giggle and broke wind. The smell made Mariella gag.

'I need a favour,' she said.

'A favour. Who the devil . . .' another giggle, '. . . do you think I am? The tooth fairy?'

'I know exactly who you are. I summoned you.'

'Yeah. And I was having a good time when you did. I was screwing some virgins. Hence the state of me. Seems a pity to waste it, good looking. Come in here next to me, and we'll make beautiful music together.' As he spoke, he ejaculated what looked to Mariella like half a pint of jism, and leered again. 'Feels good,' he said. 'Come on, baby. I'll make you come till you die.'

'No,' said Mariella again. 'I need your help.'

'I could help you in all sorts of ways.' He grabbed his penis again and shook it at the woman. 'I know you're wet. You're dying for it. And I'm just the one to solve your problem.'

'Be still,' ordered Mariella, and the beast snarled at her before doing as she said.

'There is someone I wish to dispose of,' said Mariella. 'But I don't want it to be easy for him. I want you to make it as hard as you can.'

'Nothin's harder than my cock,' said the beast. 'I'll make it hard for you.'

Mariella shot him a warning glance and the beast grimaced. 'OK, OK. You're the boss. For now.' And it leered again. 'So maybe I'll fuck this guy. Anything alive will do. And I'd keep him alive long enough to do it.'

'Do whatever you want,' said Mariella. 'And I want to know all the details.'

'Kinky,' said the beast.

'No,' said the woman. 'He killed my family.'

'Do you want a chorus of "Hearts and Flowers"?' said the beast, and mimed playing a violin. 'Spare me the sob story. I'm here, and I'm at your command. At least for now. Point me in the right direction and I'll make life so difficult for this dude that he'll wish he'd never been born.'

'That sounds good.'

'You've really got it in for this guy,' said the demon. 'And just for you, I'll make it the slowest death ever. I think I'm going to enjoy this.'

'When?' asked Mariella.

'No time like the present,' said the beast. 'Who is he?'

Mariella told him. 'Easy,' said the demon.

'Do you know where he is?'

'I'll find him. I've had plenty of practice.'

'Very well.'

'Can I go now?'

'Of course.'

'Then you've got to order me to go. It doesn't work otherwise. It's stupid, I know, but it's the tradition.'

'Then go,' said Mariella. 'Be off with you.'

And with another crash, the demon was gone.

54

Trace was still in his flat in Streatham when the demon materialized. With a bang that shook the windows, it arrived in the middle of the carpet in the living room and defecated on the shagpile.

Trace rushed in from the kitchen where he'd been getting himself a drink and reeled back from the stink, but after his previous experiences he was less shocked by the appearance of the demon than he might once have been.

The demon itself, no longer imprisoned by the pentagram, walked around the room proprietorially.

'Nice place you've got here,' he said. 'I could live here myself.'

Trace just looked at the apparition.

'What's the matter?' said the demon. 'Cat got your tongue?'

Trace shook his head, then said, 'What do you want?'

'Good question. And it could be your last.'

'I don't think so.'

'You're confident.'

'I've got friends in high places. Or should I say low places?'

'Like who?'

'I'm afraid we weren't introduced,' and Trace went on to describe the Great Beast.

'Oh *him*,' said the demon. 'You are honoured.'

'Am I?'

'Oh yes. But I don't see him here now,' said the demon.

'I've only got to snap my fingers.'

'Then do it.'

Trace lifted his hand and the sound of his fingers cracking together echoed the sound of the demon arriving.

There was a sudden hush in the room, and then the air turned red and seemed to diffuse. With a creak from the floorboards, the Great Beast arrived. He was not in disguise this time, and his head almost brushed the ceiling of the room. The blackness of his scaly skin and fur pelt seemed to take the colour out of the room and leave it almost in darkness.

He looked first at Trace, then at the demon, and nodded. 'Seems I was correct in my assumption,' he roared, and the walls shook, but no one but Trace and the demon could hear him.

'Seems so,' replied Trace.

'And you want me to help?'

'That was the deal.'

The Great Beast turned to the demon, who was masturbating furiously with rage.

'Go,' he said. 'Your powers are useless here.'

The demon spat at the Great Beast then looked at Trace. 'She's going to be very unhappy. You may have beaten her this time, but there'll be others. Luckily I won't be involved.' And with another thunderclap he was gone.

'Satisfied?' asked the Great Beast.

'No,' said Trace. 'Who is the she he was referring to?'

The Great Beast smiled, but it was not a pretty smile, and Trace blanched as the monstrous being's black lips pulled back over its pearly white teeth. 'One of your enemies. A woman whose life you devastated. You tortured her husband, then murdered her only child, a girl. Do you remember?'

Trace's heart chilled in his breast. Of course he remembered. His first mistake.

The Great Beast read his mind. 'And an expensive one,' he said.

'It was an error on my part,' said Trace.

'An error you may live to regret. I hope this doesn't happen too often. Not many of my enemies have her kind of talent.'

'For that at least you should be thankful.'

'And you.'

'I am.'

'Then I'll be leaving. But be careful, Trace, the woman has allies, and next time even I might be unable to help you.'

'I'll remember that,' said Trace, as the air shimmered again and the Great Beast was gone.

55

A second after he left Trace's flat, the demon arrived back in the pentagram in Mariella Newman's house with another ear-splitting burst of sound. She was waiting for him, sitting in her chair, her brandy untouched in her glass.

'Well?' she said.

'Sorry,' he replied. 'He's got friends.'

'What do you mean?'

He explained.

Mariella Newman tore at her hair and scalp until blood dripped down her face like a mask, and she screamed curses in her own language, and one that was even older than that.

'No need to throw a hissy fit,' said the demon. 'I did

what I could, and that's that. Anyway, how do you think I feel? I've got a reputation to keep up too, you know.'

'You useless creature,' said Mariella scornfully. 'Be gone.'

And he was.

At the factory in Peckham work went on all night, with the forensic teams beavering away collecting evidence.

Dancer, Evans and King, fortified with cups of strong coffee, stayed at the site in the portable HQ until daylight.

It was then that their first real break came.

One of the scene of crime officers came in carrying a plastic evidence bag containing a crumpled piece of printed paper.

'What's that?' asked Dancer, suppressing a yawn.

'A parking ticket,' said the SOCO. 'Screwed up and chucked in the corner upstairs.'

'Gimme,' said Dancer, and squinted at the registration number, then phoned through for a PNC check. The car was a Ford Sierra Sapphire Cosworth registered to a Paul Raymond Marsh at an address in Chiswick. It had not been reported as lost or stolen.

'And that name doesn't correspond to any on the fake ID we found,' said the SOCO.

'Didn't those firemen say that there was a Ford Cosworth parked here the night of the quake?' said Evans.

'They did,' said Dancer. 'Let's go.' And he, Evans and King hurried outside to the car.

On the way to Chiswick they were informed that Paul

Raymond Marsh had no previous record. 'Could be our man,' said King.

'Could be,' agreed Dancer.

The address was a recent conversion in a terrace off the High Street, but when they knocked there was no answer, and a quick check showed no Cosworth parked close by.

When they tried again, a young woman from the flat below came to the door.

'Paul Marsh?' said Dancer, showing her his warrant card.

'I haven't seen him for weeks,' she said. 'It's been quiet up there, and he hasn't picked up his mail.'

Dancer looked through the post. It was all circulars, nothing personal. 'He drives a very nice car,' he said.

'He does that,' said the young woman.

'What does he do?'

'God knows. Lives the life of Riley if you ask me. Comes and goes at all hours, then we don't see him for weeks on end.'

'What does he look like?'

Her description was markedly similar to that which the fire chief had given them of the occupant of the old factory.

'Thanks. You've been a great help,' said Dancer, and the trio of police officers returned to their car.

'Looks like him, doesn't it?' said Evans.

Dancer nodded. 'I wonder if we could get a search warrant?'

'On what we've got?' Evans again.

'Why not? It's worth a try.'

And it was. After very little persuasion the warrant

was signed by a court official, and the three of them went back to Chiswick with a van load of uniformed police and a dog handler.

'We're taking no chances,' said Dancer. 'If this *is* the Torturer, he's a dangerous man, and I don't want anyone walking into any nasty surprises. Who the hell knows what might be up there?'

By then it was early afternoon, and a pair of uniformed officers popped the door without much trouble, even though they soon discovered that there were three separate locks fitted.

'Shitty materials,' said one of the PCs. 'There's no point in putting a hundred-pound lock on a ten-quid door.'

Dancer had uniforms watch the back as he and the rest went upstairs to the flat. But they were disappointed. It was neat and anonymous, with no sign of recent habitation, and a close search turned up no personal papers of any kind.

'It's him,' said Dancer when they'd finished. 'I can feel the bastard. And no one lives anywhere without leaving some indication of who they are behind them. Get a fingerprint team in here. There must be dabs everywhere.'

And there were. And most matched the prints from the two previous locations where the Torturer had left his spoor.

'So what now?' asked Evans, later that afternoon.

'So now we seal the place up again and keep a twenty-four hour watch on it, front and back,' said Dancer. 'And put out a stop and detain order on the driver of that Ford. And make sure that everyone knows he's probably armed and extremely dangerous.'

56

Meanwhile the Ford Cosworth was parked in a lock-up garage a short walk from Trace's hideout in Streatham, and the man himself was sitting in the living room staring at the walls.

The news of the police find had broken in the newspapers and on TV. The full details were too terrible to release, but rumours abounded, and the electronic and print media were hinting that horrors way beyond the norm, even in this day and age, had been perpetrated behind the walls of the old factory. Trace knew that he was a wanted man. Probably the most sought after in the country, and not only by the authorities.

The woman. She was after him too. The wife of Patrick Newman, whom he had been hired to obtain certain information from, by any means. But it hadn't been Trace's fault that the bloody girl had got in the way. How in God's name had he been expected to know she'd be at home that day? It was a shame, but she had had to be terminated too. He hadn't gone there with that intention. Far from it. But she'd seen him and that had signed her death warrant. Now, somehow, the damned bitch of a mother had powers that Trace could only imagine. And she seemed to be able to find him with little trouble.

He wondered why she had not sent her demon for him when he had been at Peckham, or Greenwich, but he had no answer and dismissed the thought as irrelevant.

He spent the day wondering if he should simply run. Get in the car and head for one of the Channel ports and go abroad. He had money. Plenty of it. And a passport, in a name that was clean, hidden under the spare wheel of the Cosworth. Then, once safely on another continent, he could claim the cash in the Swiss bank account. But if the woman could find him where he was, in a place he thought was safe, why shouldn't she be able to follow him to the ends of the earth?

No. That wasn't the answer. The answer was to dispose of her before she could cause him any more trouble. She knew who he was. That was obvious. The police didn't. Or at least no name had been issued. Just the description as given by the fire chief. But if she couldn't get him one way, she could get him another. It would only be a matter of time before she realized that and gave the police a call. And he reckoned that even the monstrous being who had come to his aid before would not be able to protect him for ever from being brought to justice.

The idea of simply telling the authorities Trace's name and whereabouts had occurred to Mariella Newman too. But that was not the way she wanted it to end. Hers was a personal vendetta, and she knew that somehow, some-day, she would watch as Trace writhed in a very special kind of purgatory.

*

Trace was aware that his car had been seen by the fire crew at the factory in Peckham, and the chances were that it was on every police wanted list in the country. So instead of using the Cosworth, and after another sleepless night of turmoil, early the next morning he stole a brand new 7-series BMW from the parking lot of his local railway station. He had watched the driver park it and catch a commuter train, which, Trace figured, would mean the car wouldn't be missed until the evening. Then, with the Beretta tucked away neatly into the waistband of his jeans, he set off to find Mariella Newman.

He decided to start at the house in Kensington. He didn't know if she'd moved since the tragedy, or if she'd stayed on. But whichever, it was his only point of contact.

The crow that had been watching the flat and had followed him to the car park sensed where he was heading and should have flown on ahead to warn the Crow Man. But instead, as it saw Trace's car turn off close to South Kensington Tube station, it banked sharply and flew off in another direction entirely.

Trace parked the car on a double yellow line round the corner from the house he remembered so well, and walked the rest of the way.

It was just before nine on a morning that was shaping up to be the hottest yet, when Trace rapped loudly on the front door of the town house.

There was no answer, and he felt the sweat gather around the gun barrel stuck in the small of his back.

He hammered again at the wooden panels of the door,

and after a few more minutes he thought he heard sounds behind it. He knocked again.

He saw movement behind the glass, and the door opened on the chain, and there was Mariella Newman. Her face was still crusted with blood, her hair stood out from her head like a shaggy mantilla, and the front of her white dress was spotted with bloodstains.

'Attractive,' said Trace, as he kicked the door open, smashing the chain from its mooring.

He was fast. Faster than Mariella Newman. As she tried to speak, to cast some curse, he punched her full in the face and she tumbled to the floor, hitting her head on the wainscotting as she fell.

57

Trace slammed the front door behind him, grabbed Mariella Newman's still body by the hair and dragged her into the first room he came to. Ripping a curtain cord from the window, he bound her wrists and ankles, and stuffed her mouth with a piece of cloth torn from the hem of her dress.

Then he set off to explore the house.

He went from floor to floor, room to room, and it seemed all too familiar, especially the room where he had murdered Patrick Newman and his child. He sensed the desolation, saw the filth and neglect that his actions had caused, but he felt numb. The place stank, and the higher he climbed, the worse the smell became, until silently he crept up the stairs to the attic.

The smell was more pungent there, and he breathed through his mouth as he turned the last corner into the Crow Man's lair.

He saw the pile of festering bird corpses crawling with maggots, and the crows' droppings that hung from every surface like grey stalactites, and he saw the last of the birds that huddled together in one corner. And finally he saw the Crow Man himself, asleep on top of a pile of rags on the dusty old sofa.

Instinctively Trace pulled out the Beretta, grabbed a filthy cushion, placed it on top of the Crow Man's head, and using it as a crude silencer fired three times into the sleeping man. The Crow Man jerked like a puppet, and the thick smell of faeces mixed with the other unspeakable odours in the room as he died.

Trace turned and ducked as the crows, maddened with grief and anger, flew up and attacked him, wheeling around his head in the confined space, pecking at his face, shedding feathers as their wings beat against the low ceiling, until Trace had to flee, slamming the attic door behind him.

He stood on the stairs, wiping blood from his skin, and wondering whether to go back and kill the birds, but remembered he didn't have a spare ammunition clip, and wishing to conserve his bullets, he left them.

He went back downstairs to where Mariella Newman was waiting, conscious now, her eyes blazing with hatred.

'You've caused me no little trouble,' said Trace. 'But now your time has come.'

*

The call went through to Kensington police station. It was from a concerned female citizen of eighty-one years old who sat in her flat opposite Mariella Newman's house. The concerned pensioner spent a lot of time gazing out on to the square, but not, unfortunately, the day that Patrick Newman and his child were murdered. She'd never forgiven herself for that. The family had looked so happy, as they'd gone about their business, and the degeneration of the house had been so obvious since. All those horrible birds.

But that morning she had been looking out at the square as she drank her camomile tea, nibbling at the single slice of unbuttered wholemeal toast she allowed herself for breakfast. And she had seen the man who hammered on the door for ten minutes or more, the commotion as he'd gone in, and then the three flat bangs that sounded like gunfire. Although she was sure she must have been mistaken. But such horrible things happened these days.

The sergeant who took the call dispatched a squad car to investigate. It drew up outside the house just as Trace was deciding what to do with the woman.

Meanwhile, the sergeant, alerted by the address to which he'd sent the car, put in a call to an old friend of his who was stationed at Peckham police station.

'This is probably nothing, Jack,' he said, when the call had been routed through to the mobile HQ. 'But you never know. I know you're interested in the case, and it just seems like a bit of a coincidence.'

'Christ,' said Dancer in reply. 'Get on to your blokes and tell them to be double careful.'

But the call was never received, because the two

uniformed PCs in the squad car were standing outside the door by then.

Trace heard them knocking as he stood over Mariella Newman's still form, and he said, 'You expecting anyone?'

She shook her head.

'Lying bitch,' he said, and peered round the doorjamb at the front door.

He saw the shadowy figures behind the glass and knew they were police. 'Bastards.' He drew his gun and fired four times.

Glass exploded and slivers of wood were blown off the door as the hollow-point 9mm slugs chopped through it and ripped into the policemen standing outside, spraying flesh and blood from the exit points. One was killed immediately, but the other, wounded in the chest, managed to drag himself down the stone steps towards the police car parked by the kerb.

The concerned female citizen was watching too, and stepped back in horror as she heard what were definitely gunshots, and saw the two policemen thrown to the ground, and then one, bleeding profusely, begin to make his slow and painful way down the steps, dragging a trail of scarlet behind him.

She immediately picked up the phone and pushed the redial button.

As soon as Dancer put down his phone in the HQ, he jumped up from his seat. Evans and King were looking at him in puzzlement from hearing just one side of the conversation. Dancer moved towards the door. 'Come on, I've got a hunch this is it. I'll explain on the way.' And all three ran out to their waiting car.

Explain he did, but the explanation was interrupted by a frantic call on the radio for police reinforcements and an ambulance to be sent to the square where the shooting had occurred.

'I knew it,' he said. 'I told him to tell those boys to be careful.'

The concerned female citizen's emergency call was not the only one to be logged that morning. Several other residents had dialled 999 when they heard the shots, and the second policeman managed to get a short call in on his radio before he passed out, stretched across the two front seats of the police car in a sea of blood.

As soon as Trace fired the four fatal shots he picked up Mariella Newman and carried her upstairs to the living room that overlooked the square, dropped her on the sofa and peered round the edge of the curtains. He saw the wounded officer crawl to the police car and drew a bead on his back, but once again decided to conserve ammunition as he knew that soon all hell would break loose. A few minutes later he heard the first of the sirens approaching.

'Well,' he said to Mariella Newman, 'it looks like it wasn't such a good idea to come here after all.'

58

Mariella Newman lay where Trace had unceremoniously dumped her, and concentrated her whole being in one final effort to beat him. She knew that her time was close. She could feel it. But she would be glad to sacrifice herself, and join her family, if only by doing so she could destroy him.

She summoned up every last vestige of her powers, and prayed for the strength to do what was needed. At first nothing happened, and she felt tears well up in her eyes. Tears of frustration and tears of anger. Then, without any warning, she felt a great jolt go through her, as if she had been charged with electricity, and she knew that her prayers had been answered.

She struggled with her bonds again, but they wouldn't budge, and Trace turned as he sensed what she was doing.

'You're wasting your time,' he said. 'I'm going to kill you now.'

He looked around the room, and his eyes alighted upon a letter opener in the shape of a stiletto that stood on the dusty top of an antique writing desk.

He picked it up and felt the point, then smiled in satisfaction.

'This'll do,' he said, and approached Mariella, who tried again to free herself, but to no avail.

'Whatever happens,' said Trace, 'you'll die today.'

Thank God, thought Mariella. Because you will die

with me, and I will find the peace I've been seeking for so long.

Dancer and co. arrived twenty minutes after the first emergency vehicle had responded to the 999 calls. The narrow streets around the square had been closed and cordoned off, and uniformed police were on every corner turning away sightseers and the first media people hungry for a story.

Evans showed his warrant card. Their car was waved through and joined the other vehicles blocking the square, as far out of gunshot range as was possible. As they were parking, an ambulance trundled away, its siren screaming. That was good news at least, because it meant that whoever was inside was still alive.

Dancer went looking for the officer in charge, and was passed across to a uniformed superintendent.

'Christ knows what's going on in there,' said the man. 'Some lunatic with a gun is holding a woman hostage as far as we can ascertain. We've tried phoning, but whoever's in there just picked it up and ignored us.'

'What happened to the two PCs?' asked Dancer.

The superintendent's face darkened. 'Bad. We've got one of them out, and he's alive, thank God. But the other one's dead. A paramedic's been in and confirmed it. He's still on the doorstep, poor bastard. We're waiting for the tactical firearms squad to arrive to give us some cover. I'm not risking any more men until we've got some firepower of our own. What's your interest, Inspector?'

Dancer explained.

'And you think that this so called Torturer is the one inside?'

Dancer nodded.

'Then we've got a bigger problem than we thought.'

The superintendent was interrupted by the arrival of two Transit mini-buses containing officers armed with semi-automatic rifles and handguns, drably dressed in dark blue overalls, baseball caps and flak jackets.

Their commander, an inspector, came straight over and listened whilst the superintendent filled him in.

'First thing we do is get that man off the steps,' said the inspector. 'I'll get two of my blokes to go in and drag him out whilst the rest give them cover.'

'Then I'd like to go in,' said Dancer.

The other two officers looked at him in astonishment. 'What?' said the superintendent.

'I've been after this bloke for months. I feel like I know him. And I know the woman, too. I've spoken to her. If you send in an assault team, he'll kill her. I've got a better chance on my own.'

'A better chance to get killed,' said the inspector.

'Then so be it,' said Dancer.

'I can't authorize it,' said the superintendent.

'I've been put in charge of this case. I'm my own authority. I was told to do whatever was necessary.' Dancer was adamant.

'Including dying?' said the uniformed inspector.

'If that's what it takes. But I have to talk to this bloke. If only for a minute. If you go in, he'll die, I know it. And I'll never get a chance.'

'I'll have to get this cleared,' said the superintendent.

'Then do it,' said Dancer, turning to the uniformed inspector. 'Whilst your lot get that poor sod away.'

The inspector shrugged and went back to his men. The superintendent got on to his superiors at Scotland Yard.

59

Trace watched as the police, ambulance and fire service vehicles arrived. He saw the body of the policeman in the car taken to safety, and the paramedic check on the status of the second police officer lying in the doorway, before his corpse was removed too.

He targeted several of the individuals running around below him, but as he only had eight bullets left in his gun, he decided to save them for the inevitable show-down that was to come.

When he saw the armed police arriving, he shook his head and went back to Mariella. 'Not long now,' he said, and pushed the knife into her throat.

The pain was intense and she writhed away, but he followed.

Please kill me, she thought. Please kill me, for I know at that moment I will have my revenge.

But he didn't kill her. Instead, with the point of the knife he inflicted dozens of tiny stab wounds into places he knew would not injure her fatally.

She had never known such pain. Each wound felt as if it were full of molten steel, and tears ran down her face.

*

Dancer received permission to go inside. The head of the tactical firearms squad offered him a Browning Hi-power 9mm automatic and a flak jacket. He accepted the former, but refused the latter. 'On your own head be it,' said the man.

'It always has been before.'

'I'm coming with you, Guv,' said Jane King quietly.

'No, you're not.'

'Yes I am. There's a woman in there. I can help her.'

'Meaning I can't?'

'Not in the same way. I know her better than you. And besides, two heads are better than one.'

'Jane—'

'This is no time to pull rank,' said the young woman. 'Trust me on this.'

'If she goes, I go too,' said Evans.

'No,' said Dancer. 'This isn't a bloody charabanc outing. And you've got a family.'

'So, I can come?' said King.

'I haven't got time to argue,' said Dancer.

The boss of the tactical squad shook his head in disbelief, and the superintendent said, 'Are you sure this is wise?'

'Never argue with a woman,' said Dancer, and winked at Jane King.

She smiled back, and in her turn took the offer of a gun, but refused a body protector. The tactical inspector walked away in disgust.

Dancer and King walked together to the front door, avoiding the blood that was drying on the steps, and Dancer opened it by sticking his left hand through the broken glass and turning the handle of the lock.

Once inside, they stood in the hall, listening for any sound. Dancer noticed that he was shaking very slightly. Old age, he thought.

They checked the rooms on the ground floor. Empty. Then they started up the stairs, Dancer in the lead, his gun cocked with the safety catch off.

From the room in front of them, the one where Jane King had interviewed the bereaved woman, they heard a strange scuffling noise. The door was open, and when they looked in they saw Trace bending over Mariella Newman, who was lying on the sofa. There was blood all over her, and Trace's hands, arms, and the front of his chest were all stained red.

Dancer moved up to the landing followed by Jane. Trace looked up. 'I wondered how long you'd be. Are you all there is?' he said, ignoring the gun in Dancer's hand.

Dancer nodded, then said, 'Are you Paul Raymond Marsh?'

Trace thought for a second. 'Yes, I think I am. Why?'

'You should pay your parking tickets.'

'So I should. But that's not my only offence.'

'I know,' said Dancer, as he and Jane walked slowly through the doorway. 'We found your identification.'

'Aren't you the clever ones?' said Trace, and looked at Jane King. 'And you had to bring a woman with you. Are you scared to come in on your own?' He looked down at Mariella and then at Jane again. 'You want some of this, do you?'

'Put down the knife, Paul,' said Jane as she moved further into the room and stood next to her superior officer, cocking her gun and pointing at the Torturer's midriff.

'Call me Matt Trace. That's my name.'

'OK, Matt. Put down the knife now.'

'Fuck off.'

'Come on. This gun is loaded, and I'm prepared to use it.'

Mariella had been listening to the short conversation between the trio, floating in and out of consciousness as the pain grew too much to bear. She recognized Dancer and King from their previous visit, and wished that they'd stayed away for just a little longer, because now she knew that whatever happened when she died would include them.

'Drop the knife, Matt,' said Dancer. 'It's all over now.'

'It's never over till it's over,' said Trace, and he lifted the knife high over Mariella's still form.

As she saw both police officers' fingers whiten on their respective triggers, Mariella summoned one final burst of energy that she sent spinning in their direction, and, as the hammers of the guns fell on to the bullets in the chambers, instead of the high explosive reports that the police officers expected there were only two metallic clicks as both guns misfired.

Trace yelled in triumph and brought the knife he was holding down on to Mariella's body. As the knife cleaved her breast bone, and as she went spinning off to be enfolded by death's dark embrace, she knew that all her suffering had been worth it.

60

Both Dancer and King watched aghast as Trace cold-bloodedly stabbed Mariella Newman to death. At the point of impact, as a fountain of blood erupted from her chest cavity, Trace turned and smiled maliciously, almost as if he had known that some greater power would prevent them from interfering.

Dancer sensed Mariella's spirit leaving her body, and he felt a sudden rush of pure joy surround him, before everything in the room began to fade, the walls vanished in front of his eyes, and with a jolt, he and Jane were standing in what appeared to be a typical suburban London street. The road was broad, almost a boulevard. A double width of pavement was planted with huge old trees, whose foliage was iced with sticky dust after the long, hot summer. It seemed maddeningly familiar to him, as if he had been there before, but he could not remember when, and there was no street sign to help his memory.

The road seemed to be completely deserted. Not a soul stirred, and there were no cars parked along either side.

Dancer looked at Jane in mystification.

'Where are we?' she said. 'What's going on?'

Other questions filled Dancer's mind as he stood there looking at his companion. What had happened to the house in Kensington? Where was Mariella Newman's body? Why had both their guns failed simultaneously?

And more importantly, where was the man who'd said his name was Matt?

But if these questions were not disturbing enough, the thing that worried Jack Dancer the most was that when he looked down at the road beneath his feet he noticed it was not paved with tarmac but with tiny yellow bricks.

'God knows,' he stuttered as he tried to take in the situation, and find some point of reference that made sense.

Jane King tried to work the action of her automatic, but it was frozen solid, as if the metal had been welded together. Dancer's was the same, and they holstered the useless weapons.

The air around them was as thick as syrup, and smoggy. It stunk of petrol fumes, and the cloying scent from the trees.

Immediately, Dancer felt sweat break from every pore, as if he'd stepped fully dressed into a sauna. He saw from the perspiration that had broken out on Jane King's face that she felt the same. At least that was something to hang on to.

The sun was like a huge orb of liquid fire in the sky, its edges haloed with the muck from the atmosphere, and the sky itself was a cloudless, navy blue bowl that seemed to hang only inches above the roofs of the huge houses standing in their neatly tended grounds.

Dancer studied them one by one for any sign of life. But they all stood four square on their foundations, silent as tombs, with their blank windows reflecting the sun like mirrors.

He noticed two things almost simultaneously; two movements that disturbed the uncanny stillness of the afternoon. Firstly, high in the branches of a plane tree a hundred yards down on his right, were three massive crows, their plumage shining like it had just been oiled and polished, their beady eyes focused on the street. He saw them move on the branch in an agitated fashion as, from around the next corner, Matthew Trace strolled by, the bloodstained knife stuck in his belt, and the Beretta in his right hand.

Dancer pulled Jane back behind the shelter of another huge tree and they watched as Trace approached.

Trace also saw the birds, but not the two police officers. He was as confused as the detectives. All he knew was that he was free, and he assumed that the Great Beast had once more intervened on his behalf. But as he saw the black birds, and remembered the crows that had attacked him in the attic in Kensington – and the others that had kept appearing in his life – he wasn't so sure. Instinctively he aimed the gun up into the tree. It felt heavy and deadly in his grasp, the metal warm to the touch. The butt of the gun was wet and sticky with Mariella Newman's blood. He held it with both hands to keep the weapon steady, aimed at the crow on the right and fired.

The gun jumped in his grasp, the sound of the shot deafening in the hot, still air as the bullet found its target, ripping flesh from bone, and blowing the body of the bird off its perch. It tumbled through the leaves and branches to land on the pavement with a soft splat, followed by a flurry of coal-black feathers floating slowly down to the ground. The other two crows rose from where they were sitting with a flap of their huge wings, and a rusty cawing echoed around the silent street.

Trace smiled to himself. Not so tough, are you? he thought, as the two birds disappeared behind the turrets of a mock Elizabethan mansion.

Then he saw her.

In the distance, through the heat haze that rose from the surface of the road, a tiny figure appeared.

He knew who it was, even though she was hundreds of metres away.

Nadia Newman.

He stood confused for a second.

How could it be? he wondered.

But it was. As she came closer he knew it for a certainty. She was small, just as he'd last seen her. And she was dressed exactly the same as the day he had killed her.

As she advanced towards him, her bare feet making no sound on the yellow brick surface of the road, he saw her nightie with the embroidered teddies around the neck, stained with deep red blood, just as it had been when he had left her lying on the kitchen floor of her family's apartment.

Suddenly he was frightened.

For the first time in his adult life, he knew what fear was, and part of his brain told him how his victims must have felt when he worked his unique skills upon them.

'Stop,' he said, and his voice trembled and sounded strange inside his own head, like an old fashioned radio when one of the valves had gone.

'Stop or I'll shoot.' His voice became stronger, more confident, as he raised the Beretta.

*

Dancer and Jane had seen her too. From their position behind the trunk of the tree, they watched as she got closer, and they knew who she was, although they had never seen her, either alive or dead, except in photographs of the murder scene, when even there her features had been hidden by a mask of dried blood.

They could also see what Trace intended. Jane King made a move to come between them, when a voice whispered in her ear, 'Don't.'

The two officers' heads turned sharply, and they saw Mariella Newman standing beside them where an instant before there had been no one. She was wearing the same white dress that had been in tatters around her body as she had died on the sofa in Kensington, but now it was whole, her body free of all injuries, her hair was thick, dark and lustrous, and her face was that of someone in her mid-thirties, not the hag-ridden woman that they had seen on their brief meeting.

'Don't,' she repeated, and smiled. 'What must be, must be.'

'But he'll kill her,' said Jane King.

'No. No one really dies.' And Mariella touched the younger woman's arm and held her still, then held Dancer's arm with her other hand, and all three watched as the drama unfolded before their eyes.

Inexorably, Nadia kept coming.

As she got closer Trace saw that her eyes were wide and unblinking, the particular shade of cornflower blue that he could not forget. Her hair was long and straight, and shone blonde in the sunshine, but the ends of it were stained red from the gaping wound that he'd made in her throat. The wound that had finally killed her.

The wound was bleeding freely, as were the others he had inflicted on her small body, and the pale blue of her nightdress was marred by the wet, red stains.

'Stop,' said Trace, almost sobbing, for the third time. 'Right now.'

But still she came, and he squeezed the trigger of the big automatic. The first bullet struck her just beneath the breast bone on her left side. The thin cotton of her nightdress dimpled slightly as the bullet hit, and chunks of flesh and bone and cloth blew from the exit wound in a shower of blood. But, although she hesitated, she still kept advancing towards him.

He fired again, his hands shaking, and the second bullet slammed into her right shoulder, splintering the bone, and sending another spray of red to splatter on to the pavement. But once again, she kept coming.

His third bullet cut her left leg from beneath her, shattering the thigh bone and cutting the muscle. This time she did fall, only to drag herself closer using her fingernails and one good leg for leverage. And all the time she looked at him with her huge blue eyes, and never spoke a word, or made any sound of pain.

When she was only a metre or two away, with her nightie filthy from the ground, and a trail of blood glistening on the roadway, Trace forced his hand to be steady and fired at her head.

The bullet tore through her skull, splitting it like a ripe melon, exploding splinters of bone and a thick gruel of blood and brains all over her body.

Only then was she still.

Trace stood with the gun in his hand, the metal hot from the shots he had fired, his arm trembling with the strain of aiming it, and its recoil.

Dancer and Jane had watched in horror as the bullets cut the young girl down, but her mother's hold on their arms, as light as a feather, but as strong as steel hawsers, had prevented them from intervening.

Trace leaned against the fence of the house closest to where he was standing, marvelling that no one had come out to see what all the commotion had been about, when from behind him he heard a soft voice.

'You can't kill her again,' said the voice. 'It doesn't work that way.'

Trace spun round, the Beretta held out at arm's length, to find a tall, cadaverous figure standing in front of him, dressed in a dusty black frock coat, black stove-pipe pants, white shirt, and an incongruously old-fashioned top hat. The man who had spoken was old. His face was as lined as a Tube map, and thin white hair stuck out from under the brim of his topper. It was the man that Trace had shot three times in the head in the attic of the house in Kensington.

But that's impossible, Trace thought. He was dead, he had to be. His skull was blown to pieces with three heavy-calibre bullets.

'As impossible as the fact that Nadia is not dead either,' said the figure, reading Trace's mind.

'Who are you?' said Trace.

'They call me the Crow Man.'

'And I *have* killed her,' said Trace.

'Have you?'

Trace glanced round. Where Nadia's body had been,

the street was empty. There was no sign of her, or the thick soup of gore that had stained the ground.

From their vantage point, Dancer and Jane King watched in amazement as all signs of Nadia disappeared with a pop, and simultaneously the old man, who they had not seen before, appeared from nowhere. They turned to Mariella, a million questions on the tips of their tongues, and she smiled again, shook her head and taking her right hand from Jane's arm placed the fore-finger on her lips. 'Wait,' she whispered.

'Here she comes now,' said the Crow Man to Trace. 'How many bullets do you have left?'

Far away in the distance, Trace saw the tiny figure of Nadia advancing towards him again.

He spun back to the Crow Man and fired once. The old man's body simply absorbed the bullet. After a second he spat the lump of lead from his mouth into his outstretched palm. 'I used to do that in the music halls in the twenties,' he said mildly. 'Isn't it a shame that they're all gone? I blame television myself.'

That was when Trace broke. Up until then he'd been able to handle what was happening, but no more. He dropped the gun and ran.

'You're wasting your time,' said the Crow Man, as Trace ran up the pathway to the front door of the closest house and began to hammer on it.

There was no answer, and as he looked back down the path he saw Nadia and the Crow Man standing at the gate looking at him. One of the remaining two crows had settled on the Crow Man's shoulder and was clean-ing out his ear with the tip of its beak.

Trace turned tail and ran again, watched by Nadia, the Crow Man, Mariella, Dancer, and Jane King.

And then the most horrible event of all the horrible events of the day began.

61

It was the season of the flying ants.

The hot weather that had lasted for so long had hatched their eggs early.

At first there were just a few. Dancer and Jane saw them oozing out of cracks in the pavement and from nests in the dirt under the tree where they were standing. Then there were more. Scores, hundreds, thousands. Little winged, black-carapaced insects that blindly crawled over each other, heading for the light of the sun.

And finally there seemed to be millions of them, coming from everywhere, and as if on some prearranged signal, they lifted like a dark, winged carpet and flew.

They flew in Trace's direction, ignoring anything and everyone else in their path.

As he ran from the Crow Man and Nadia, the ants pursued him.

He looked over his shoulder and saw them, and the look on his face was one of pure terror.

He ran fast, his arms and legs pumping like pistons, but the ants were faster.

They caught up with him as he crossed the front lawn of the house, and attached themselves to his body, covering him like a suit of black. They swarmed over him, forcing themselves into every orifice; filling his nose, mouth, eyes and ears until he could no longer see, hear, speak or breathe.

Each of the millions of ants that attached themselves to him had a sting in their tail, and a tiny sucker there to draw out blood. Rows of tiny teeth inside their mouths chewed up the meat that they fed upon.

And they were hungry.

They stung his clothes and bare skin, blindly pumping tiny drops of poison against anything they felt. When they smelled blood, they slurped it up. When they found flesh, they bit into it.

He opened his mouth wide to scream, but as he did so, more ants filled it, and stung and bit the delicate membranes of his throat and tongue.

They went down into his lungs and up into his sinuses. They forced their way into his inner ear, and on into his brain, all the time stinging and feeding. They stung his eyes until he was blind, and chewed at the delicacy that were his eyeballs until they were gone; and the ants that had devoured them pushed on into his brain too, eating the live matter as they went. They stung every centimetre of his flesh and sucked out his blood until almost every drop was gone. The sheer weight of them slowly forced Trace to his knees, ripping at the ants that were devouring his face with fingers as fat as sausages from the insects that clung there. Then he fell backwards, and lay on the soft carpet of grass as the ants stung him to death. It seemed to those watching to take for ever.

But finally, when they were done, the ants rose like a cloud and flew away to digest the blood they had sucked out of his body, and the meat they had eaten from his bones.

Dancer looked round for Mariella Newman, but she was gone. He looked back to where the Crow Man and Nadia had been standing, and they were gone too.

He never saw any of them again.

The street was silent. The ants were gone, and the only evidence of what had happened was Matt Trace's body, lying where he had fallen on the lawn of the house, drained of blood, with empty sockets where his eyes had been, staring sightlessly up into the sun.

That, and Jane King standing next to him, her hand on her mouth.

'Are you all right?' he asked.

She said nothing, her eyes still on Trace's body.

'Jane,' said Dancer.

Still no reaction, and he caught her arms and turned her round to face him.

'Jane,' he said again.

Her eyes stared vacantly at him.

'Sorry, love,' he said, and slapped her round the face as hard as he could.

Her eyes came back into focus, he saw recognition cross her face, and she threw herself into his arms, sobbing helplessly. He embraced her clumsily, patting her back until her breathing slowed and she stepped away from him. 'What is happening?' she said.

Dancer shook his head, walked across the yellow brick road, through the open gate, up the path and across to Trace's body.

But as he got closer, and saw that Trace was not much more than a skeleton inside the clothes he had been wearing, and that he was indubitably dead, the landscape began to shiver, and Dancer saw the walls of the house in Kensington begin to take shape in front of his eyes again, and he fainted clean away.

62

Jack Dancer never worked again. At least not as a police officer, although the years that were to come found him in many strange situations. But few as strange as on that hot summer's afternoon in the house in Kensington, and in the familiar suburban street which he was never able to find again, no matter how hard he tried.

When the tactical firearms squad cautiously entered the house after hearing nothing from him or Jane King for thirty minutes, they found him lying on the carpet of the first-floor living room, and his female companion standing, leaning against the wall next to him, her face a complete blank. Dancer was alive, but barely, and was rushed to the intensive care unit of the Chelsea and Westminster Hospital, where he stayed, clinging to life for the next two weeks. Jane King, who at first refused to answer any questions, was sent to the psychiatric ward of the same hospital, but discharged herself the next day.

Mariella Newman was dead on the sofa, her body dreadfully mutilated, but her face was serene, and she seemed to have regained the youth she had lost since her family had been murdered.

Both officers carried holstered handguns. Unfired. When they were later tested, they both worked perfectly.

In the attic, the police found dozens of dead crows in an advanced state of putrefaction, and the old sofa that stood in the centre of one of the rooms was heavily bloodstained. But no body was anywhere to be found.

Of Matthew Trace, there was no sign.

When Dancer recovered sufficiently to answer questions, he insisted that he had spoken to the Torturer, and that he was no longer any danger to society. He refused to expand on the statement, and asked to be considered for early retirement. His request was granted. Jane King, meanwhile, had disappeared.

Then, one afternoon, she came to visit him in the private room he had been moved to from the ICU. She brought the usual fruit and flowers, but all he really wanted was a cigarette, and after it was lit he said, 'Jesus, Jane, where have you been?'

'Around.'

'They told me you'd disappeared.'

'I have.'

'Does anyone know you're here?'

She shook her head.

'I guess I blew it, Guv,' she said. 'I reckon I'll be on permanent suspension from now on.'

'Me too,' said Dancer, and explained about quitting. 'But you're only young, Jane. You've got your whole career ahead of you. You shouldn't let it go just for this.'

'What am I going to tell them?'

'The truth.'

'And get sectioned? It took me hours to get out of the loony bin they'd stuck me in as it was.'